Esther Pein

The Migration of the Geese

by
Hildegard Horie

Many thanks to Ken and Luella Hillmer for editing this book.

ISBN 978-0-557-11073-5

Table of Contents

I don't like this   5

The village store   19

Jan   26

Esther Pein visits the old people's home   32

The move to the old people's home   42

The first day in the retirement home   46

If the dear neighbour doesn't like it   52

The child and the shadow   65

Mrs. Raiman   72

The Christmas market   75

An idea becomes reality   89

Problems are getting bigger   94

My Dodo doesn't want me   97

Helena   102

Visit at the hospital   107

One Day Only   109

Mrs. Pein as match-maker   112

Christmas preparations   118

The Eternal Today   120

A home coming   124

Back to everyday life   129

The trip   137

A new perspective   147

Miss Baumgarten   152

The migration of the geese   159

Farewell from the old people's home   161

I don't like this

It was early October. The sun painted the leaves of the park with a golden colour. Esther Pein carefully put one foot before the other. Since her fall a couple of months ago she did not feel stable anymore and had started using a walking stick. The leaves rustled like parchment underneath her feet. She had reached a little pond and sat down on a bench, her stick between her knees was enveloped by her long skirt. Her bony fingers were holding on to the knob. She leant back and took a deep breath. The sun played in the white hair and gave them a silvery shine. But Esther Pein did not know this. She looked into the blue sky and followed with her eyes a bird with large wings drawing circles. Then she closed her eyes. A soft breeze touched her cheeks and played with her hair. From the church tower near by there came twelve dull strokes. Esther Pein heard them and yet she did not hear. The last stroke was still hanging in the air when a young couple came hand in hand.

"That's a nice spot you have found here," while the young lady said that, her white teeth radiated. Her cheeks were glowing and her long blond hair touched her shoulders.

"Yes, indeed," Esther Pein said.

"Don't catch a cold," the young man added while passing.

"Don't worry, I'll take care that I'll keep warm from the inside."

The young couple laughed, grasping their hands even more firmly, chatting joyfully. The red sweater still could be seen from a distance. Esther Pein smiled, when she saw how the young girl started to jump, pulling her friend after her. Everything was peaceful on this sunny day. Life was good. "It's worth living," Esther thought. "It all belongs together. Being young and getting old."

At her feet two sparrows were fighting for a few crumbs with outstretched wings. Esther bent forward,"Wait-wait, who wants to fight on such a day. The whole park is yours, and you have to fight exactly here?"

With her right hand she fumbled in her skirt pocket and pulled out a plastic bag, that was closed carefully. Now with the help of her left hand she untied the knot. "Because it's such a nice day," she said, while breaking a small piece of the bread crust. Immediately a gray-blueish dove appeared and snatched away the bread. The sparrows were frightened and gave way.

"Who told you it was meant for you!" scolded Esther Pein and took another piece. This time she threw it immediately in front of the sparrows. Again these little birds started to fight. "So wait, I have enough for everyone!" the old lady said and watched amused how the little crumbs were picked up by the little beaks. "To be honest, this bread was meant for the ducks," she said and took the stick from between her knees and got up to get closer to the pond, where a group of ducks lazily glided on the calm water. From time to time one of them dived the colourful head deep into the water so that the surface cracked into thousand pieces.

At that moment a young child around four years old came running, pointing excitedly to the ducks. Esther Pein gave her a piece of the bread.

"There you are, Helen! I was afraid you would not come today. Do you want to feed the ducks?"

The little girl reached out the hand cheerfully to take the bread and carefully threw it into the water. Immediately the first ducks snapped the piece. The girl looked up waiting.

"Yes, of course, I do have more. Plenty. But this time you have to throw it much further."

The girl nodded, took the bread and threw with all her force as far as she could, then turning to her Mom, "Mama, Mama, they have swallowed every bit."

The mother was now standing beside Esther Pein.

"We are late today. There was a celebration in Kindergarten."

"I already missed my little friend. It's strange how quickly you get used to something."

"Yes," said the young mother. "This pond is like a magnet for Helen, and I believe, not just this pond," she added smilingly.

"I must admit, I forgot your name."

"Hanna Venicetti."

"Of course! Maybe that's because of getting older. But your name, young lady, I'll never forget!" She stroked her hand over the black curly hair." Do you want more?"

Helen jumped excitedly from one leg to the other and stretched her little hands out. This time it went even better than before. She raised the little arm as high as she could and threw with all her might, then looked at the old woman, who shook her head laughing, "That's all. If you are coming again tomorrow, I'll give you more. O.K.?"

As if the little girl did not believe it, the small hands were still outstretched, waiting.

"You heard, what Mrs. Pein said, come!" She grabbed the hand of her daughter. The girl turned once more and followed the ducks with longing eyes before she finally tripped along with her mother. Esther Pein went slowly back to her bench and closed her eyes.

It was good to feel the sun in her face, like a caress. All her muscles relaxed. For a moment she forgot everything. Suddenly a bike stopped beside her.

"Finally I found you!" the voice was reproachful.

Mrs. Pein was startled. Among thousands she would have recognised this voice. She opened her eyes and looked into the reddened face of her daughter, who embarked from her bike and positioned herself challengingly before her mother.

"What do you think - if you are thinking at all! I looked for you everywhere!"

"You have? I am sorry to hear that," Esther Pein said innocently.

"Did it not even cross your mind that I would look for you?"

Mrs. Pein shook her head somehow helpless. "No, really, this thought did not even cross my mind. It was so beautiful out here."

Her daughter touched her forehead with her left hand, imitating her mother's voice mockingly, "It is so beautiful out here..." And she started to scold her mother. "Didn't you think I would be worried? When I called home and nobody answered I got worried. I left everything at school to hurry home. I was afraid something would have happened to you. And when I arrived home, you weren't there."

"Of course not, I was here!" Esther Pein said laughingly.

The daughter looked at her mother bewildered. "I can see that!" She shook her beautiful head so the brown curls were shaking. "I was about to call the police!"

"But darling, this is a bit overdone, don't you think?"

"You can easily say that! I feel responsible for you, can't you see?"

"How often did I tell you already that I am old enough to take care of myself."

"Is that so? Then you forgot what the doctor said? He had ordered strictly bed rest for you."

"Did he?" the old mother asked surprised.

"Not only that. If you wouldn't obey he could guarantee nothing, he said."

The old mother shook her head. "How strange, did he really say that?" She looked at her daughter with her brown innocent eyes.

"What you don't want to hear you don't hear." The daughter turned away angrily. "Are you coming or not?"

"Please, let me stay a bit more. It's so beautiful out here."

"Listen mother!" her voice was stern, "I don't have time to run after you. I have other things to do!"

The mother got up slowly. "You are right. I should have told you. I did not want to make you worry, Britta, do you believe me? I thought, because it's so beautiful outside today and the whole week it was raining..." She did not finish the sentence, tried instead to keep step with her daughter.

At first the daughter mounted the bike to drive slowly ahead, then she got off again to push the bike. The old mother could sense that her daughter was angry.

"Don't be angry with me, Britta, I really did not want to worry you."

"It's always the same! Sometimes I think it's easier to take care of little children, than of your own mother!"

"But I told you, you don't need to take care of me."

8

"And if something happens? Hm? Then it's me who has to live with a bad conscience for the rest of my life."

"You don't need that, really you don't." The old mother was out of breath and had to rest for a few seconds.

The daughter did not say anything, only shook her head. The distance between the two grew. Britta tried to walk slowly.

"I am coming, you can go ahead. I know my way," the old mother said.

Finally the daughter mounted the bike and drove away. Mrs. Pein stopped again and followed with her eyes a squirrel that jumped from branch to branch. The little animal stopped for a while, looked around, the bushy tail trembling and then it disappeared.

"If only I had a peanut," Mrs. Pein thought. "Next time I have to take some peanuts along." She was about to look for the little animal, when she remembered her daughter. No, she should not make the situation worse.

"Next time!" she called after the squirrel,"but you have to remind me, otherwise I'll forget!" She smiled and continued walking.

When she arrived at her house, the bike was leaning against the garden fence. Her daughter was not there. Mrs. Pein opened the garden door and walked carefully over the gravel. The flowers were withered. Only some dried stumps reminded her of the past beauty. On the cherry tree there were still some red leaves like drops of blood clinging to the naked branches.

"The garden surely asks for work. If only I could do it like before," she murmured, "No, Britta can't do everything. I wish I could help." She tried to pick up some dried branches.

"Mother!"

Frightened she dropped the twigs.

"I told you not to do that!"

"Now listen, Britta, can't I do anything?"

"I have to talk to you." The voice of her daughter became business like.

"Go ahead. I am listening."

"Not here."

"Not here?"

"At first I wanted to tell you tonight, but now I can do it all the while I am here."

"This sounds exiting." The old mother tried to smile.

"I know, you won't like it..."

"Is that so?"

"Yes, I know. But I don't know what else to do. I talked with aunt Lilly and she too said this would be the best solution. Otherwise she would have taken you to live with her, but her children are coming for a visit, therefore she does not have the space."

"Now go ahead, what is it?"

They had reached the entrance door. Britta turned the key and opened the door. A bright ray of sun flooded in and touched the stair case. The old mother leant her walking stick against the railing, took off her coat and hung it in the wardrobe, then she bent down to unleash her shoes, holding on to the railing with her right hand. Her daughter watched her. For a moment it was as if she wanted to help her mother, but then she turned away and walked with firm steps into the kitchen. The old mother slipped into the house shoes.

"This all came unexpectedly." she could hear the voice of her daughter from the kitchen. "I did not think it would happen."

Mrs. Pein waited. "What is it?" she asked finally.

"A colleague of mine has offered me a position in Chicago."

"Chicago?" Her voice trembled. The old mother was leaning against the kitchen door.

Britta opened the fridge and pulled out a basket with vegetables. "At first I did not want to accept, because I did not know how you would react." She took a cabbage and got rid of the outer leaves.

"But why Chicago? That is Wild West. There you are not safe anymore."

"I am not on my own. Herbert is coming with me."

Esther Pein startled. "Herbert? Who is Herbert?"

Britta took a large knife and a wooden board and started to cut the cabbage into small pieces. "You don't know him."

"Do you know him?"

Britta laughed a bit too loud. "Would I go with him otherwise?"

"But Chicago. Why of all cities Chicago?"

"There are reasons."

"Who is this Herbert?" the old mother asked again.

Britta fetched a white plastic bowl and put it into the kitchen sink.

"You will get to know him one of these days. As soon as he is free, we want to marry." She rolled her sleeves up, put the cut cabbage into the bowl and filled it with water.

"What do you mean, as soon as he is free? Is he married?" she asked, suddenly getting suspicious.

"That is not exactly what I would call it. He has been working out a divorce for more than a year." Britta washed the cabbage and poured out the water.

"And then you want to travel together, you and he?"

"Sure."

"You don't know him long enough."

Britta emptied the bowl into a cook pot and put the pot on the stove.

"Listen mother, I am grown up, am I or am I not?"

"Sure you are, Britta. I am only interested. I mean, it's always good to know each other over a longer period of time until you go places together."

Britta dried her hands and turned to her mother. "Times have changed, mother."

"No, Britta, there are things that never change."

"We are not living in the eighteenth century anymore."

"No, we are not living in the eighteenth century anymore, in that you are right. But there are certain things that don't change."

"That's a matter of opinion." Britta turned away abruptly, took an empty plastic bowl, opened a drawer to fetch some potatoes and started to peal them under running water.

"Britta, I don't like this at all. You should think about your daughter."

"Anette is eighteen years old. She has her own life."

"This could be, Britta, in spite of this she needs you. She needs a home. Do you know what she told me before she went to the States? Omi, since papa left, I don't have a home anymore."

Britta was silent.

"Sorry, Britta, I did not want to hurt you."

"It's o.k."

"Is this all you wanted to tell me? Or is there something else?"

Britta bent to fetch the second pot from the cupboard, turning her back to her mother. "Then came the question what should become of you."

"Of me? Oh, don't worry about me. I can busy myself."

"No-no, you can't stay here on your own! You know that quite well, after your heart attack I can't let you be on your own. The responsibility would be too big. Yesterday I visited the *Sunset House. House of Peace* was all full. There was not a single room available, only in the *Sunset House* I was able to get a room."

"Sunset House?"

"I admit, it does not sound appealing, but it should be nice, I was told, it has nice furniture. And the manager was - - in the beginning she told me, every room would be occupied and she would not have a space - "

"The manager was what?"

Britta became angry. "I only talked with her over the phone, and when I explained the situation she became more friendly. I am so relieved that it is possible."

"Possible what?"

Britta fell silent and put the pot with the potatoes on the stove.

"Did she offer you a job? Then you don't need to go to Chicago? Britta, this would be a different perspective. You often complained about the work load and that everything in school became so inhuman and hectic. I am glad for you that you have found something else!"

"Either you don't understand or you don't want to understand! It is because of you!"

"Me? But I told you, I am fine here where I am."

"Mother, now listen. You can't stay in this house on your own. That is impossible. If something happens when I am away - - I can't take you along with me."

"But darling, don't get exited! I absolutely don't understand why you are so worried about me."

"Now listen. I have a place booked for you."

"For me?"

"Yes, for you."

"Without talking with me?"

"Only for the time being."

"For what time?"

"These weeks when I am in Chicago."

"Weeks? Which weeks?"

"From Nov. 3rd to May 6th."

"Nov. - Dec - January - February - - "

"You will be surprised how quick time flies."

The old mother did not listen anymore. "These are - - these are more than 6 months!"

"What are six months!"

"And here you were thinking all this time how to get rid of me and didn't tell me anything. You were making plans without including me. Sure, you are including me, only the difference is, that I had no idea and you were deciding over my head about me."

"Mother!"

"I understand. Oh yes, I do understand quite well! The question is, if I agree with this agreement? Treating me as a child."

"But you would never have agreed."

"Of course not! What do you think!"

"I did not have a choice."

"I can stay here on my own."

"The risk is too high. Then I would not find a single minute of peace, neither day nor night."

"I can ---"

Britta felt helpless and hurt, but at the same time angry. "I can see, you are only thinking of yourself. You don't care that I have not seen my own daughter for more than a year. I finally would like to do something which I like to do, this does not interest you either. This shows how selfish you are!"

"I could go to - - "

Britta turned to her mother: "Could go where? Na? To whom? Would you like to tell me that? Your siblings are all dead. You don't have close relatives either."

"That may be. But 6 months - that's a long time."

"If you are looking ahead, maybe. But I could not shorten the time. Herbert said that an old people's home is a good thing."

"Herbert said so?"

"And if you like it there, you could even stay there. I talked with the manager. Believe me, you are in good hands."

Esther Pein sat down on her chair. "Old People's home, how does that sound!"

Britta took the electric water kettle and poured water in and plugged it in. Then she took two apples, one orange and a banana and started to peel the apple. "One day you have to face reality."

"So? I have to face reality? Which reality?"

"That you are not fifty anymore."

"Oh, this I know already. But thanks for reminding me! I have something to do."

Mrs. Pein stood up slowly, but soon sank back on the chair.

"You are a stubborn old woman." Britta started to cry, threw the apple and knife on the counter and banged the door.

The old mother shook her head. "How stagy! Can't she talk reasonably about such a plan?"

The steam lifted the lid of the kettle and spit out white foam. The water sizzled on the stove element. Mrs. Pein got up to reduce the heat and put a wooden spoon underneath the lid, so the steam could escape. "A stubborn old woman - do I have to listen to such rudeness? Don't old people have any rights anymore?"

She went to the door. "Britta!"

There was no answer. Mrs. Pein stepped in front of the window and could see her daughter taking the bike from the garden fence, getting on the bike and driving away.

"An old stubborn woman... This I don't need to accept. She could have told me quietly." Then she stopped and thought again and started to talk to herself. "Would you have agreed with it? Of course not! I don't see any reason why I should go into a home for old people as long as I can manage on my own. So, what else could she have done?" Mrs. Pein stared in front of her. The water kettle started to hiss. The old woman pulled the cord from the plug and left the kitchen. She climbed the few steps up to her small apartment.

In the bird cage hopped a canary excitedly from one stake to the next. The old woman remained in front of the cage.

"Did you hear that, Hansi? She wants to put me in a home for old people so she can go with her Herbert to Chicago. And she doesn't even know him. I should be concerned about her and lock her in."

The little bird listened attentively, holding the little feathery head lopsided looking at her with its black pearl eyes. Tschiep-tschiep. "I knew you would understand. But what would become of you? That does not concern her." Tschiep-tschiep. "Oh little feather ball, what do you know? You don't know what it is getting older. You are getting old without realizing it. Maybe only outsiders can see it. And then they decide what to do. Old people don't have a say. But I am not old, not yet. And you too know that I am not that old, do you? In your eyes I am still young. I am telling you stories every evening and you are singing a special song for me, or even two. Are we not a unique pair? What is she thinking? What would she say if I would make decisions for her over her head? Why do young people always think they could take control over the old people? I won't go, Hansi. Do you hear me? The two of us will watch each other. I bring you fodder and keep your cage clean and give you fresh water every day and you are entertaining me with your song."

Mrs. Pein went up and down in her room, then stepped in front of the window and looked outside. A foam of silver was spread on top of the branches. Drops were glittering like diamonds. She looked from one piece of furniture to the next. She had learned to love all of this. This was her home. The large clock in the corner, reaching from the bottom to the ceiling with the two hanging pendulums. Underneath the window was the love seat and sofa with the little table. At the wall the cupboard with the old porcelain, even her own grandmother had used it. Across at the other wall was the

Ibach piano. It was long ago that she played on it. Years ago, when her husband was still alive, they often played together. And then all these books, who had been with her like old friends over all those years. The small kitchen was only separated from the living room through a low dresser. Even here she had everything she ever needed. On one board hand painted old mugs were hanging. Every piece had its own history. And the bath. It was so easy to reach. And then the bedroom. It was a perfect little apartment without steps. Warm. Bright. Friendly. And all this she should give up? Changing for a room somewhere? She let herself fall in the comfortable rocking chair and tried to think. She thought for a long time, until the sun disappeared behind the mountaintop. The sky was painted with a faint red colour. Was somebody there? She listened. But everything remained quiet. She only could hear the up and down hopping of the little bird. She was about to turn on the old floor lamp but then decided otherwise. She sat back in her rocker and remained without moving and let her thoughts run freely.

"Stubborn old woman! She should not have said that. No, this she should not have said." She realized how she called this feeling back again and again to wound herself each time anew. Finally she got up and went into her little kitchen busied herself at the fridge, but she had lost her appetite. "Stubborn old woman" played constantly in her mind and she decided not to eat anymore tonight. "That's all her fault," she murmured. Suddenly she started. "Listen, Esther, you are grown up and still acting like a child. She has hurt you and you want to take revenge and hurt her in return. Is that not childish? Is it not her right? She feels closed in and would like to free herself. She would like to enjoy life, but she can't because her mother is home and nobody there who takes care of her. Besides, she wants to visit her own daughter. Would I have done anything different? A daughter who does not have a father anymore. Or what is even worse, she has one, but one on whom she can't rely on, who does not care."

Mrs. Pein stepped to the wall where the calendar hung. "What did she say? From November 3rd to May 6th. There is Christmas in-between. The first time we would not be together at Christmas. That she did not mention. She would like to celebrate Christmas - this time without her Mom."

Her fingers fumbled from one week to the next. She counted the days. Then the year ended. She did not have the new calendar yet.

She could hear the key in the door and waited. She listened how the door was opened and closed again. She heard hasty steps along the corridor. Then silence again. Shortly after that she could hear the television.

"Britta is home," Esther Pein thought and went into the living room.

"Stubborn old woman - this I don't need to put up with," she murmured. She flipped through some magazines, but did not know what she was looking for.

In the bird cage it was quiet. The little bird sat on one leg, ruffled its feathers like a feather ball. The little head deep in the feathers.

Her fingers fumbled for the switch. A moth fluttered against the lampshade.

"Stubborn old woman- -" she listened again. The television was silent. Mrs. Pein sneaked quietly out of her apartment. Only a few steps separated her apartment from her daughter's. She kept the door open so enough light could brighten the steps. Carefully she felt her way to the door.

"Britta?"

No answer. Carefully she opened the door and was startled. Britta was sitting at her desk with her head on the panel.

"Britta?"

The daughter straightened up.

"Are you crying?"

She wiped her eyes. "It's o.k."

"Listen, I have thought about it. You are right about the stubborn old woman, you are absolutely right. I was very selfish. I have only thought about myself and not that you could have been worried. I counted again. What does is mean, just a few months? You should not give up this idea because of me. You should enjoy this time. And if I can do something for you, let me know.

Britta jumped up and embraced her mother. "Forgive me, I should never have said that! I was so disappointed, so disappointed."

"I do know, Britta. But now we can talk about it. Have you eaten something?"

"It's almost seven, Mom. I have been home in the meantime."

"I did not hear you," Mrs. Pein said. "And who will take care of all the flowers if we are not here?"

"Miss Wild our neighbour said she would do it."

"You talked with her already?" There was again a strange tone in her voice.

"She offered it. First I had asked my friend Ellen, if she could live here in the meantime. But she wanted to visit her own kids. Then I asked Linda, but she too had other plans and so had Pat. I even thought of putting an ad in the paper, but you never know whom you will be stuck with. Then Herbert had the idea with the home."

"So, that was Herbert's idea?" Mrs. Pein became reproachful again.

"Who is this Herbert? Can't you tell me?"

"I told you, you will meet him."

"Is he an older man already?"

"Just four years older than I."

"Is that so. Four years older than you. Does he have children?"

"Two sons. They are married already."

"Do you know what you let yourself into?"

"You don't need to worry about me, mother."

"That what you think. Don't let's talk about it now. You are old enough. Listen, Britta, I am going tomorrow morning to see the home. I just want to have a look for myself. Where is it?"

"Maybe at the weekend, then I can come along. It's not far from here. only maybe half an hour by car"

"Those few months - - this we can handle, don't you think so?"

The village store

When Esther Pein woke up the next morning, the sun touched the colourful comforter of her bed. Beside her the regular tick-tock of the alarm clock could be heard.

"Nine o'clock! How could that be!" She took the clock to make sure she read correctly. But she could clearly hear the tick-tock.

Britta is at work already, she thought and folded back the bed cover, then sat on the edge of the bed. Her knees were painful. Instinctively she started to massage, then she got up to go to the bathroom. Suddenly she was fully awake. Had it been a nightmare or is it reality? Sometimes she could not distinguish between dream and reality. Did she quarrel with her daughter last night? Slowly she remembered. They wanted to put her in a home for old people, like a useless piece of furniture.

She had to admit at 82 she was not the youngest anymore, but strong enough to remain in her own apartment, but her daughter had made up her mind already to get rid of her. As if it would be her responsibility to take care of her mother. Responsibility she called it. The word burden she did not use, at least not in the presence of her mother. She wanted to go to America and she only could go if her mother was taken care of somewhere else. Mrs. Pein took the towel to rub her skin, then sleeked the hair with the brush. She looked into the mirror. Somehow she got used to the sight. Only sometimes she was surprised, wondering if this really was her or maybe somebody else?

She went into the kitchen to prepare breakfast, when she realized that she was out of bread. It was good that the village store was near by. She put on her shoes, took her coat and went to the shed to take out the bike. This all happened mechanically. She was about to mount the bike when a sharp pain stopped her. Then she remembered that she was not allowed to ride a bike, at least not now. She put the bike back and closed the door of the shed.

"I can walk just as well," she told herself and realized that she had left her walking stick at the house. "It's not that far, just a couple of minutes," she said to herself. Still she felt insecure but she did not want to go back again, that she did not want either.

A visit at the village store was always something special. Her life did not have many highlights anymore, just tiny bumps, but even they were important to her. In earlier years, when her husband was still alive, everything was different. They could go to places together and spend their holidays there. Since he was no longer there, it became more quiet around her. Her daughter moved in with her and took the lower apartment. This happened quite natural, and besides, it was the cheapest solution. There were difficult years before the divorce, not only for Britta, also for herself. And of course for Anette. The child was at that time just 12 years old. They cried a lot. Mrs. Pein shook her head. "Don't think back. What had been done, had been done," she said to herself. Britta went back to her former profession. As often as Mrs. Pein watched her daughter Britta she had to admit that she was born to be a teacher. Only recently she became more and more aware that all the stress was becoming too much for her. It was good to be close together, only sometimes she wondered if it was a good decision or not. They both were so different. The biggest difference was, the one was young and the other old. Years back everything was different. There she was fully occupied, not only in the house and the garden, but she had the feeling she was in control of life. Things that were so normal once now became a real challenge. In addition to that there was the pain. She shook her head: "Pein, no self-pity," she scolded herself.

At the right and left side of the street apple trees stretched their naked gnarled arms toward the sky, as if calling for help. On the meadow sheep were grazing. A truck turned from a side street and rattled past. The big wheels hurled black clumps of dirt on the street. Mrs. Pein stepped aside and waited.

"I still have time, all the time I need, as much time as I could wish for."

Ten minutes later she had reached the little village store. She was surprised to see so many people. The little room was packed with people. All people she knew.

In this village everybody knew everybody. And if anybody had missed some news, here was the best place to be filled in.

The melodious tinkling of the little bells was still hanging in the air, when they approached her with the latest news.

"Our store is about to close."

"The store? Our store?" Mrs. Pein thought she had misunderstood. Then she remembered having seen the large sign in the window: *liquidation sale*, in large print. She had seen it, but did not pay any attention to it.

"It is said they can't continue since the new supermarket had opened in the neighbouring village."

"But this is impossible! This store was here first," Mrs. Pein protested and stretched her posture as if ready to fight such injustice.

"That's what we said too."

"Is there nothing we can do?" Mrs. Pein turned to the portly owner and asked again, "Is there nothing that could be done, Martha?"

They all called her Martha.

The woman shook her head. "I even went to the mayor."

"And if we all start a de - - de - -" Mrs. Pein looked around helplessly, "how do you call this?"

"Demonstration."

"Yes, if we all get together in a demonstration, you know with flags and banners and so. And then gather signatures from everybody in this village..."

"It would not help a bit. Believe me. They do what they want. And they have the money. The Big-ones kill the little-ones."

"But we did not try." There was this tiny spark of hope.

"And who is doing the work?" the stout woman behind the counter asked with a low voice. The grey curls were no longer able to cover the bald spots on her head. Dark shadows framed the deep seated eyes. She looked worried. "I am not the youngest anymore. I wanted to give up two years ago, but nobody was there to take over."

Mrs. Pein thought for a while, then she said, "and there are so many without a job. Should we not find somebody who is unemployed? At least for a couple of hours a day?"

"And this is a fine store. You can buy everything you need," an elderly woman in a blue scarf said and pointed with her arthritic finger to the full boards. These boards were filled with noodles and rice, coffee and bread and sweets, cheese, sausage, butter, milk and yogurt, and in the large deep freezer you could find ice, frozen vegetables, pre-cooked meals and meat, and under a half glass cover on top of the counter fancy cakes and pastry, on which a fly was creeping and enjoying the flavour. On the floor there were boxes with bottles. And underneath the window large baskets with various fruits. You could even buy nuts. Also children should not go empty handed. There they could find games, puzzles, crayons and dolls, cars and aeroplanes, even all kinds of zoo animals, and in the lowest board you could find teddies in all colours and sizes.

"There is nothing you can't find here," the old woman in the scarf repeated.

"And it is so convenient. If you forgot something, you can come back within a couple of minutes without using your car," another customer added, who carried her baby on her back. The little one slept, the tiny head lay peacefully on her mother's shoulder.

"That all is true, but still there is nobody who could take over," the owner said in a low voice.

"And what if we all - I mean, if each one of us here - - " Mrs. Pein had not finished the sentence, when she realized it was not a good idea. Would she be ready to be here every day for a couple of hours? She had to admit, this would be too much for her. At that moment she realized that she was not young any more. Much of what she had taken for granted she just could not do anymore.

"It's not only that," the store owner said, "such a big store can sell everything cheaper. With this stock here there is not much you could earn in the first place. It is hardly enough to pay taxes."

Mrs. Pein looked unhappy, then she closed her brown eyes for a moment as if deep in thought, asking for advice from her inner self. But as much as she tried to find a solution, there was none available. At first she was tempted to say, "I'll ask my daughter," but at the same time she knew this would not make a difference.

"I really do hate the thought," she said finally, "this store is like - like my mother. Older than I am. When we moved here, this store was here already. It belongs to my life. It's a piece of myself."

"I do understand your feelings, Esther. Many feel the same. My grandparents started this business. But time changes. The big stores swallow everything. Fifty years. Believe me, that is not easy. Fifty years. But I am not getting younger either. I am seventy-two. Tomorrow I will be seven-three." She leaned against the counter as if she was looking for support. "I sometimes asked myself, how long I could continue doing this."

Now everybody tried to comfort the store owner. At that moment the door was opened. The tingling of the bells drowned out the murmur of the voices. An older gentleman his shoulders bent forward stepped in. At the same time a small black and white cat rushed in and rubbed gently against Mrs. Pein's leg.

"Why should the big-ones with the money always win?" asked a little old woman, who was sitting on a chair beside the door. She was an old farmer. Her face was marked by deep furrows. And when she talked you could see that her teeth showed many gaps.

"With all the whys no battle was won so far. We have to come up with a plan," said another white haired gentleman. They all knew him. He was the teacher of the little village school for many years. When finally the school closed he did not move away.

"Come up with a plan - but what kind of plan? You heard, there is nothing we could do."

"We have to write to the government."

"They have more important things to do than to care for our little village store." This was Heather Walter. In her youth she was politically very active, but now she was retired. "I do know, believe me. We can't expect any help at all from them, maybe just before an election."

The old gentleman who had entered the store a couple of minutes ago, put his cap on the counter. "What is going on, if I may ask?" he said politely.

"The store owner explained. The gentleman thought for a while, then he said, "Life is full of changes. We can't hold on to the past, even though we would like to."

23

"That's easy to say. But what should become of us?" The voice of the old farmer's wife trembled.

"At first it might be difficult. In a couple of years it belongs to the past. Changes belong to the human growth process."

"Human growth process," repeated Esther Pein sarcastically to herself, but did not voice it loudly enough so anybody could hear. Suddenly she remembered the talk with her daughter. "Stubborn old woman" - was this kind of change also sort of a growth process? Whatever, she did not want to think of it now.

Finally Esther Pein bought a few buns, and - as if she had to comfort the owner - she added butter and yogurt - and a teddy.

As soon as she stood outside the store holding the huge teddy in her arm, she was wondering why on earth she had bought this teddy.

Then she thought of Helena. Had she not promised to come again to the pond? She hastened her steps and realized that something like joy sprang up in her.

When she arrived home she did not take off her coat and shoes, just sat the huge teddy on the lowest step of the staircase, put the yogurt and butter into the fridge, then took a few dried bread crumbs out of the wooden box and put them into a plastic bag. She looked at the clock. Eleven thirty! It's time, otherwise I will miss the little one. She grabbed the teddy and held it firmly under her arm. She was about to leave the house, when she stopped, then turned around to fetch her walking stick and closed the door behind her. It started to rain. Tiny pearls stuck to her coat. The sky was covered with a grey blanket. Nevertheless she continued to walk. She could already see the pond. But she could not see any human beings.

"Maybe she will come later," Mrs. Pein thought. She was about to sit down on a bench, but in the meantime the bench was so wet, that she had to wipe it with her handkerchief. It started to rain heavier. She tried to cover the teddy with her coat and looked in that direction where Helena and her mother usually came. The clock on the nearby church tower stroke twelve. Still nobody was in sight. She had the impression as if she could hear the gay laughter of the little girl. She waited another ten minutes. Then she turned to go home. The rain left dark puddles on the ground.

She was close to home already when she realized that she still had the bread crumbs in her pocket. "Then tomorrow," she told herself. Maybe it's good that she did not come, it's better to give the teddy for Christmas anyway," and she was surprised that she did not think about that before.

When she arrived at home she started to shiver. She took the teddy and sat it in the corner of her sofa. "As if he belongs there," she said amused. She took off the coat and put it on a hanger to let it dry, stepped into the slippers and put on the heater. Then she remembered she had not even fed the little bird. She stepped to the cage.

"Hi, little fellow, you might think, what on earth has happened to this old fool? Is she already that far gone that she forgets her best friend? But to be honest, you could have said something, instead you did not say a peep. And look how dirty the cage is! That all comes because they want to close our village store. Our whole life is upside down. You see how important it is that everything remains the same as always. But on the other hand, if we have the courage to accept a change, we remain flexible. What do you think? Of course, you agree. You are such a clever little thing. I would not know what to do without you. And what about you? Without me? Probably you would not like this either, wouldn't you? One gets accustomed to each other and at the end we believe we cannot live without each other's company. But maybe that's an illusion. There are many illusions. Only sometimes we want to hold on to such illusion."

She poured kernels in the little bowl and renewed the water. "So now your little world looks different again: fresh water, in the bowl some seed - that's life how it is meant to be. Only some clean sand for the bottom is missing - but not today. Next time."

As if the little bird wanted to show that it agreed, it jumped into the tiny bath and started to flap his wings so the water spilled all over. Then it hopped on the upper stake and shook its feathers. Peep-peep! Without waiting for an answer, it hopped on the ground and started to pick some seeds.

"Surely, always first the sunflower seeds," Mrs. Pein laughed, "that's right. And what is left does not taste so good any more. Maybe canaries are not that different from people."

25

For a moment she stood in the room not knowing what to do next. The whole day belonged to her, and she did not know what to do with all that time. Jan came to her mind. She had not seen him for days. "I will go to see him," she decided.

Jan

Jan lived in a little house on the edge of the forest. Everybody knew him and tried to avoid him. Some were afraid of him, others did not know what to do with him. Jan had always lived in this village. His parents and grandparents had lived here. The big field beside Jan's place belonged to his brother Harald Walther. But his own brother kept distant from him. Being the mayor of this village it seemed to be beneath his dignity to have a mentally challenged brother. Only his younger brother Charles came from time to time for a visit. Jan loved his "little brother" as he called him. He admired him.

When Esther Pein first met him, he was a young man of about twenty. She still remembered when she saw him for the first time. He was on the way to the field to milk the cows. He was riding his bike and behind him on the two wheeled rattle trap he had huge metal milk cans. It was as if she could still hear the rattle of the empty cans. Some schoolboys stepped in his way, making faces at him and started to laugh. Jan stopped sharp and jumped from his bike to run after the boys. The bike fell and the cans ended on the road with a loud bang. Finally Jan returned scolding loudly. In the following night he screamed and raged that she could hear it at her home. It is said, three men were not able to hold him. They called a doctor who gave him an injection, so he would quiet down. Only much later she learned his story.

He was about two years old when he received an vaccination against smallpox virus. After that he got a very high fever. Nobody knew what really happened and the doctor did not want to tell the parents.

However, the parents soon realized that something had changed. He was not like other children. He was different. Through the vaccination his brain had suffered. His speech was slow and the expression in his face showed clearly that he was not like other people. But he was not stupid, even though he had difficulties learning. He read a lot. Only he could not control his emotions. Even though he had to take medicine all his life, it happened frequently that he got a fit of raving madness. This resembled an eruption of a volcano each time it came. Then it was best to keep distant from him.

Mrs. Pein had experienced it several times when he had screamed through the night and threw things. One day when he had such a fit she was in the garden. She dropped the spade to see what happened to him. There she saw him in his workroom, boxes strewn all over the place, paint pots emptied, the window was broken and glass on the floor - it was chaos.

She stood there paralysed and asked, "Jan, is there anything I can do for you?" He stared at her in sheer unbelief. The baseball cap had fallen from his head, the blond hair was hanging in his forehead, huge pearls of sweat were running down his face. In his raised hand he was holding a chromium plated coffee pot, which he was about to throw against the wall. He let down his arm. Foam came from his lips. His small eyes were flickering wildly.

"Jan, come on, sit down and tell me what happened," she had said calmly. And what she herself did not expect happened, he came closer and sat down on the wooden bench. With her sleeves she brushed away some broken pieces of china and sat down beside him. She put her arm on his shoulder. He let it happen. She could hear his hasty breathing.

"Did they tease you again?" she asked. "If I see this happen, I promise, I will explode. Then you don't need to. O.K.? They are stupid children, sometimes even the adults. They are just stupid. And stupid people you can't change. It would be best to ignore them." He did not say anything, just staring in front of him.

"May I come to visit you from time to time?"

He nodded, while his blonde hair strands were covering his forehead.

"Shall we do some cleaning up?" she asked.

He did not say a word.

"This is a nice place. A real workroom." Mrs. Pein got up and looked around. "What is that?" she asked and took a wooden figure from the ground. One arm was broken. "Did you make this?"

He was silent.

"You did. Tell me, you are a real artist!" She stooped down to get the broken arm and pressed it where it used to be. "Can you repair this?" He still did not answer. "This is a masterpiece! The face, these fine lines, as if he would be alive!"

"I have more of those." He got up and stepped in front of an oak cabinet and opened the door. On the shelves were many figures of animals and people.

"You have made all these? You know, you could make a lot of money with that!"

He was silent again and he stroked the hair away from his forehead. Then he stooped down to fetch his cap and put it on.

"I wish my daughter could see that!"

He took one of the figures and gave it to her. She gave back the broken figure and looked at the other one in his hand. "What a gracious posture of this doll," she said admiringly. "Where did you learn that?"

He grinned proudly.

"I am not an expert but this, I can see, is a master piece. And the plaits. Did you have a pattern?"

He stepped to the commode and opened a drawer and took out a book. Esther Pein placed carefully the figurine on a board and took the book. *The art of carving*, she read aloud. Then she found the model.

"Jan, you are an artist, indeed you are."

"It's yours," he said.

"You mean - "

He nodded.

From that moment on their friendship was sealed. And that was more than twenty years ago. Since the properties were side by side, they saw each other nearly daily. Often he came and then they drank a cup of tea together and chatted. As if she did not have anything else to do, she visited him to tell him everything, that had happened in the neighbourhood. Most of the time he was in his workroom. He only went for the night to sleep in his little house. It was a small house, the one room was bedroom and living room and kitchen in one. Most of the time he spent in his workshop.

In the little iron stove the fire was still roaring. The plate was glowing and the water kettle was humming. Next to the stove wood was piled up. And on the wardrobe was a radio, still playing.

"Jan, nice seeing you!"

He turned towards her and grinned over his whole face. Esther Pein came closer and took a three legged stool from underneath the large wooden table and sat down.

"Did you know that they want to close our village store?"

He put aside his carving, turned his baseball cap around, sat halfway on the table and let his legs dangle.

"I did not know."

"This will be a big change for all of us From now on we have to go to the big city far away. And not everybody in this village owns a car. That means, we have to take the bus or the bike. But in winter this would not be that easy."

"There they say, the technique would help us to save time - but that's not true. We have less time than before."

"Yes," said Esther Pein. "Fortunately I do still have my bike, but for how long, I can't tell. And the traffic is getting worse."

"You said a bus is going?"

"Three times a day. In the morning twice and then again in the afternoon. That isn't nice either."

Jan thought for a while, then he said, "I could go along with you."

"That's good to know, Jan, especially in winter. I don't like to go out if it's icy and slippery."

"When will it close?"

"I don't know. Soon, I assume. Everything is already on sale. There is a large sign in the window, liquidation sale. To see that, it really hurts."

"Yes," said Jan and looked sad.

"There is nothing stable in this world. I would like to hold on to what I am used to."

Jan nodded. He understood. Over the radio came an announcement and immediately after that sport news followed in a hectic voice. Jan got up to turn off the radio.

"And something else. I am supposed to go to an old people's home."

Jan looked at her in shock. "Old people's home? You? But you are not that old, are you?"

"That what I thought - until yesterday. But do you know how old I am?"

Jan shook his head.

"Guess."

"I don't know. One hundred?"

"Not quite! Some years are still missing. I am going to be 83."

"I would not have guessed it. You are still riding your bike."

"That's true. But my daughter won't let me anymore She is afraid I could have another fall, like before. And I must admit, since the heart attack I don't feel safe anymore."

"But why a home?"

"Only for the time being, Jan. My daughter is going to the States and does not want me to be in the house on my own."

"But I am here."

"That's what I thought too. If something would happen, I could call you. But in the night, that's something else."

"I can come over to sleep in your apartment, if your daughter doesn't mind."

"I don't know, Jan. She made up her mind, so it's better I do what she wants. There is a nurse on duty all the time. The hospital is around the corner, and there is always a doctor. Here in this village there is no physician."

Jan did not say anything but she could see that he was thinking.

"Jan, I came to tell you that. Probably I'll need you. I don't know how to get over this. I don't like the thought at all. I would prefer to stay here. Here everything is familiar and convenient. I am scared, to face something new, Jan. If somebody is that old, you don't get accustomed that easily to a different surrounding and everything. Then you would like everything to stay as it is."

30

"Is there nothing that could be done?"

"I thought a lot, but I don't have a solution."

"What if I come along with you, I mean to the home?"

"That would be a different story." For a moment her expression brightened.

"Could I bring along my workshop?"

"I don't know. I don't know the house at all. Besides, I guess it's pretty expensive."

"How much?"

"You won't believe it, but I forgot to ask my daughter. Good that you asked. I have to find out this evening, when she comes back."

"I could come along, Mrs. Pein. But maybe they don't want me." His eyes showed a sad expression. "I know already, that they don't want me there. You are the only one who wants me. And my brother Charles."

"Will you help me, Jan? I believe without your help I can't cope."

Jan nodded. "Sure, I'll do what I can."

That night she dreamt. She was living in a huge palace. The entrance hall was packed with people, old people, young ones, they all were excited and talking at once. At first she did not understand what was going on, then she found out that the palace should be destroyed. She thought about where to go and she was wondering what would become of all the clutter she had gathered through all these years. She went from one room to the next. It would be impossible to take all that along. At that moment her mother came in. But she knew her mother had passed away long time ago. "My child, this is all just dead weight. The earlier you let go, the better. Only then you are free."

Esther Pein was about to protest, when she woke up. Her heart was racing. Could it be that the closing of the village store meant that much to her? Then she remembered the home. A hot spark of fire flashed through her. It was already ten o'clock. Did she really sleep that long? This never happened when she was young. The days always started early in the morning. Maybe she should postpone the visit to another day. This would all be too much. She realized a dark cloud was settling down on her mind. She had difficulties breathing.

"I have to eat first," she thought and went into the kitchen to see what she had in the fridge and then was wondering what to cook for lunch. But to cook just for herself? She did not feel like doing it.

Finally she took a slice of bread, spread some butter on it and plugged in the water kettle. It was still raining. The telephone rang. She took the receiver.

"Mother?" this was the voice of her daughter. "I am coming right away, just to let you know, so you are prepared. You are ready, I hope?"

"Of course, I am," she heard herself answering.

"Could you prepare something for me to eat for lunch as well?"

"I will do that, Britta." Her voice became stronger.

"I love you, Mom."

"I love you too, child."

Mrs. Pein held the receiver a long time. What more did she desire ? "I love you, Mom..."

Esther Pein visits the old people's home

Britta had cleared the dishes. She briefly examined her mother.

"You can't go like that!"

Esther Pein looked up in surprise. "Why not? What's wrong?"

"It does not fit. A flowery summer dress and this yellow jacket, this does not fit. And besides, it's the end of October. And yellow and your white hair, that does not match."

Esther Pein looked at her daughter in her green striped blouse, the narrow fitting jeans and the sneakers. "This does not fit either," she thought, but did not say anything. She went to change. Shortly after that she came back.

"Do you like me now?"

"That's better," her daughter said and dried her hands. "I will be back in a minute." Her movements were firm and quick.

"When I was her age, I was the same," she thought, "everything was different."

"Mother!" she heard the voice of her daughter calling her impatiently. "I am waiting!"

The old mother hastened not to let her daughter wait. The motor was running.

"You know, getting older has its advantages as well. It can be even quite nice," she said when she sat beside her daughter.

Britta did not say anything, but concentrated on the traffic.

"Somebody else is in charge," she continued.

"I can't see how that can be nice." Britta said shortly. "I prefer to drive myself."

"Because you don't trust?"

Britta briefly looked at her mother. "Maybe," she said smiling, "but not only that. It's the feeling of having the steering wheel in your own hands. I can't stand it, when Herbert tells me how to drive. "Watch out!" "Now turn left, now right. It's red, can't you see?" Britta laughed. "Maybe the other way around it's the same or maybe even worse."

"There is so much we have to learn, as long as we live. There is not a single day that can't teach us something new."

Britta did not say anything. They drove in silence along the wide avenue. At both sides the large trunks of chestnut trees were lining the street. Mrs. Pein knew this area very well. When her husband was still alive they used to drive along here often.

"The next rain will soon take away the last leaves, but then it won't be too long until everything is covered with a white blanket. Like in a fairy tale. And underneath this white blanket of snow new life is waiting. What a miracle! Every year." Britta did not say anything, she remained silent.

When there was no reaction, Mrs. Pein looked at her daughter. "She does not hear me," she thought. "Her mind is somewhere else. Maybe with Herbert."

"I love autumn," the old mother said and opened the window. "The soil smells differently than usual." Britta still did not listen.

33

Then the old mother gave up and fell silent. The traffic came to a halt. Britta hit the brake and drove slowly to the curb. By now she seemed to be awake.

"It looks like a funeral. I never saw so many cars here."

Mrs. Pein felt uncomfortable. "Here it is?" she asked with a timid voice.

"Probably on the other side. One of these houses."

Immediately ahead of them a car left and Britta took the chance to take the space. When the old mother remained unmoved, Britta became impatient.

"Don't you want to come?"

The old mother examined the long row of houses. "You mean - here?" Her voice trembled. In secret she had hoped to find an old shack with damaged window glass and a pile of garbage in front of the door to have a reason to go back.

"Are you sure?"

"No. 608," she heard the voice of her daughter. The house with the red roof and the little porch."

Cars passed constantly, so Britta had to speak against the noise to be understood. "Come!" she called her mother and put her foot on the zebra crossing.

The house was located on a busy road with maple trees. Here too most of the trees had already lost their leaves. A cold wind shoved the leaves across. Britta gave a sign to the drivers that they wanted to cross and waited. But one car after the next ignored her signal. Finally one car stopped. The old mother tried to walk as fast as she could not to upset her daughter, but in the middle of the street she had to stop, to get air.

"Watch out!" Britta screamed and pulled her mother away. A car nearly touched her.

It was a heritage villa. Surely it had seen better times. Still one could guess the former beauty, but time had left its trace. Britta opened the iron gate. They entered a little front yard. The roses had lost their beauty already. Broad steps of stones led to a covered entrance door with greyish, striped columns, decorated with a border of stone roses. The big sign above the door showed that they were at the right place. In bold letters they could still read - even though the writing was fading: *Sunset House.* The entrance portal consisted of two wings, each wing with long, narrow windows behind iron bars. Britta pulled the curved knocker at the left. A tinny rattling of the bell echoed through the long hallways. They waited.

"Shouldn't we better return?" the old mother asked timidly.

Instead of an answer Britta rang again. Finally they could hear steps. A key was turned. A thin lady in a black dress and a white small cap observed them from head to toe.

"What's it about?" she asked with a nasal twang.

Britta explained briefly, but before finishing, the lady said, "For that we have visiting hours." She pointed to a board that was pinned on one of the columns.

"But - -"

"You can come next Monday at 11." With that she was about to close the door, but Britta put her foot in the space.

"We have an appointment."

"Appointment? With whom?"

"Somebody told me I should come this afternoon at three. Because of formalities. During the week I can't make it."

Hesitantly the lady let the two visitors inside. "Wait here."

Mrs. Pein sat down on a wooden bench right beside the door. The back rest was artistically carved with animal figures. Mrs. Pein thought of Jan. She leaned her walking stick against the wall, but slowly the stick glided and fell with a loud bang on the flagged floor. The echo sounded through the long corridor. Mrs. Pein tried to reach her wooden helper with her feet to draw it closer, but she pushed it even further away so it became more difficult to reach. Britta bent down and gave the walking stick back to her mother. "This time better keep it in your hands," she whispered.

Mrs. Pein looked around. It resembled a reconstruction. Left from the entrance was a separate room with a speaker window, This apparently was a new invention. Still she could see the black labels from the company. A long runner was rolled up, blocking the entrance to the bureau. On the right hand of the staircase there was an elevator.

Approximately five minutes had passed.

"We are not welcomed here," the old mother said and startled when she heard her voice echoed, then continued in a whisper, "If you ask me, this is not a good sign."

"There are everywhere good and bad days," answered Britta also in a whisper.

Finally the lady appeared again, showing them with a move of her head to follow her. After a few steps she stopped. "Turn right, the third door to your left." She herself disappeared in the opposite direction.

"Thanks," Britta said.

"For that she says thanks," the old mother thought, but did not say anything. She followed her daughter. The floor was dark. Only from the far end a small light fell through a tiny round window with lead decorations, close to the ceiling. Britta was looking for the light switch but could not find it. At the third door she knocked.

Behind the desk was a stout elderly woman with a woollen pullover. Tiny grey curls covered her head. She looked over her bifocals and listened to what Britta said. Then she pulled some forms out of the top drawer and shoved them to Britta.

"When you have finished filling this out, leave it here." That said she busied herself again with some writings.

"Excuse me," Mrs. Pein dared to interrupt the busy lady, "can I see my room, please?"

"That's not possible. Unfortunately."

"But I would like to see the room," Mrs. Pein insisted.

"I told you, that is not possible. All rooms are occupied."

The lady continued typing into a computer, from time to time shuffling through some papers.

At that moment a middle aged lady in long brown-green checked slacks and a red jacket entered. The black hair was tied in a knot. Mrs. Pein could see immediately that this was not the real colour, since the white already showed through. Her lips were emphasized with a pink colour. Her face showed deep lines. From her ears dangled round silver rings. She realized that there was some sort of a problem.

"New here?" she asked with a deep voice.

"Yes," said Britta quickly.

36

"I would like to see the room before I agree to come here," said Mrs. Pein with a timid voice.

"Of course. Just a moment."

The lady stepped in front of a huge black board with many keys and numbers, where all the rooms were registered. Mrs. Pein watched her and saw that the black colour was no longer covering all the white hair underneath. The lady turned to the secretary. "Give the key from room 210. The couple in 210 are away over the weekend."

Reluctantly the secretary got up to find the key with a big metal knob. Mrs. Pein was about to reach for the key, when the secretary gave the key to Britta, not without giving Mrs. Pein a strange stare. Mrs. Pein murmured something that nobody understood.

"On the second floor, left," the lady with the black knot said and took some papers from the desk. Before leaving the room she turned to Britta, "I was about to go there myself. I am Mrs. Liebreich. With whom do I have the honour?"

Britta introduced herself and her mother.

"Mrs. Pein?" repeated Mrs. Liebreich.

"Pein with an e, not with a."

Mrs. Liebreich looked up but did not say anything.

"I am coming as soon as I have filled out the forms," Britta said.

Mrs. Liebreich went ahead. The old mother could hear the clacking of the high heels on the scrubbed tiles and was eager to keep pace. When her walking stick hit the tiles she was startled and quickly pressed the stick under her arm not to cause any noise. She felt uncomfortable in the company of this lady. To bridge the tension she asked, "Are you the mother of the house?"

The lady turned to Mrs. Pein, smiling somehow ironically, so that her small lips became even smaller. She pressed the button of the elevator.

"I would hardly call me the mother of these old folks. I am the owner of this house."

Mrs. Pein did not say anything. One could hear the opening of the elevator. Mrs. Pein felt even more uncomfortable.

"A bit narrow," she said.

"Narrow? This is good for six!"

Mrs. Pein regretted having said anything. With a sharp jerk the elevator stopped. The seconds stretched until finally the metal gate opened. The hallway was dark. On the left and the right were closed doors with numbers. Mrs. Liebreich put the key into one of the keyholes and opened. A sticky air met them. Mrs. Liebreich opened the heavy curtains and switched on the light, but still it remained dark.

"Is that my room?" Mrs. Pein asked.

"I can't tell yet. But all rooms are alike. Here nobody should feel second place."

Somehow intimidated Mrs. Pein looked around. A huge television screen filled one of the corners. In front of the television was a green sofa. Two twin beds formed a 90 degree angle with a night console. Mrs. Liebreich straightened the bedcover. The pillows were put a certain way so two tips were pointing straight upwards. The red roses on the pillows did not match the pattern of the bedcover. On the wall with big flowery wallpaper was a picture with a heavy metal frame. Mrs. Pein looked at the picture and started to shiver.

"It's winter the whole year," she said. "I should not have said that," she thought.

"We can't change our pictures all seasons," Mrs. Liebreich said.

"Of course not."

Mrs. Liebreich pulled a plastic curtain aside. "The basin. The toilet is on the same floor, just opposite." Then she opened a small door, "a little room for storage."

"Will I be alone in my own?"

"Most of the rooms have two beds, others have three. We do have a few single rooms as well."

"I would like to have a single room with my own toilet and bath."

"My goodness, we are not a luxury hotel on the Riviera, we are an old people's home!"

Mrs. Pein murmured something.

38

"What did you say?" asked Mrs. Liebreich.

"It's O.K." Mrs. Pein stepped in front of the window to look outside. The small square backyard was closed in with a high stone wall. Inside the yard were garbage cans flowing over. Newspapers and Pop cans were strewn around. Some boxes stacked together. Also a bike without rims, as well as a dented bucket and some paint pots. On the opposite side was the grey wall of a two storey duplex with tiny windows. At that moment Britta entered the room, looked briefly around without saying anything.

"I would like to bring along my own armchair." Mrs. Pein pointed to the easy-chair, that was standing right underneath the window. The pattern was hardly to be seen and the colours already faded.

"P-l-e-a-s-e, mother!"

"The rooms are furnished as they are. We can't make any exceptions. And so far nobody has complained."

"What about the pictures? Can I at least bring my own pictures?"

"Mother, p--l--e --a--s--e!"

"The walls are not supposed to be damaged. Any questions?" Mrs. Liebreich played impatiently with her keys.

"I would like to see some other rooms as well."

"But I told you already, they are all the same."

"I mean the dining hall and library or what else."

"Alright, if you insist. Follow me."

In leaving the room Esther Pein saw a Bible verse framed above the door, *Don't be afraid, the joy of the Lord is your strength.* "I can't sense any joy in these walls," she thought, "or was it just irony?" But now was not the time to think, Mrs. Liebreich was waiting already in front of the elevator and blocked with one hand the mechanism.

They stopped one level lower. Along the hall way old people were waiting. Some of them were sleeping. Others were talking. Now one of the nurses appeared, pushing a wheelchair. It was the same person who had greeted them at their arrival. Without saying a word she pushed the wheelchair close to the wall and fastened the brakes, then she disappeared again. Mrs. Liebreich opened the glass door.

"The dining room. At 5 supper is served."

"At 5?" Mrs. Pein asked.

Mrs. Liebreich did not pay any attention to the question and continued the tour. Esther Pein looked briefly around. The long tables were set horseshoe-shaped and filled nearly the whole room.

"These are no real flowers," the mother whispered, "I can see, they are not real."

Britta did not answer, hurried not to miss Mrs. Liebreich.

"Here the gym, but it is not used." The room was empty except for one stationary bike. The long narrow windows nearly touched the ceiling. There were no curtains. In a big box she could see some colourful balls and a hoop ring. On top of a table was a recorder.

Mrs. Liebreich turned into another hall way. In one of the niches were two little chairs with a low table and a lamp. On top of the table were some magazines. *Our Home* Mrs. Pein could decipher while passing.

"The lounge and visitor room."

It was a large room with a high ceiling. From the ceiling a chandelier was dangling. In one of the corners was an old woman with a young blond lady and a five year old child. The child was bored and pulled her mother's hand.

"That's all. When are you coming?" Mrs. Liebreich asked.

"I'll let you know. Probably in the beginning of November," Britta said.

"How many people are living here?" Mrs. Pein asked.

"Forty, sometimes forty-two. At the moment forty-one. More questions?"

"The kitchen. I would like to see the kitchen."

"Our house guests are not allowed to enter the kitchen. Something else?"

Mrs. Pein was silent. Mrs. Liebreich briefly bowed her head and left. One could hear the clatter of her high heels.

"I have two options", Mrs. Pein thought, "either I say NO or - - " but did she have a choice? "If I go, I'll do it for Britta's sake. To please her. Not because I would like to. It's far better where I am right now. But for her sake. Surely there are other homes in town, but they all were occupied as Britta told me. You have to make reservations years ahead and then hope that somebody dies... It's only temporarily. Maybe sometimes you have to do something even if it does not please you. And how much is Britta sacrificing for me. She could have an easier life, if I would not be in her way."

"Mother?" her voice sounded unhappy. "What do you think?"

"What I think? You really want to know? Britta, I am sure, there are nicer homes around, and nicer people too - but let's give it a try. Maybe there is a hidden purpose behind all this. Maybe. I don't know. But somehow - somehow - - I think it tickles me to find out why it is as it is. It resembles an enchanted castle. I think, I should go. And besides, what are a couple of months? I will have enough to do. It's clean. That's important. I would not call it modern and with comfort, but what you need is there. And what is it that a person needs?"

Britta pressed the hand of her mother. "I am proud of you, mother! And I promise you, I'll come back as quick as possible. And if you can't cope with it, call me."

They were about to get into the car, when Mrs. Pein looked at her daughter.....

"Britta, one thing we forgot to ask. How much?"

"2,500 a month."

"2,500? But this - this is impossible!"

"You can't get anything for nothing anymore."

"But 2,500!"

"There is everything included. All the meals, heat, water, washing - everything."

"What do I eat. It's not much. It's not that expensive. And my pension is not that high!"

"Also the cost for a nurse is included.

"And if I don't need her?"

"Nevertheless."

"But Britta, I can't afford that."

41

"I will pay part of it."

"Imagine what we could buy with all that money! That is - - 15,000 for a few months!"

Britta did not say anything.

"With that much money we could finally buy a new heating system. We always put it off because we did not have the money."

"This is more important now."

"Is there no cheaper place?"

"Other homes were double. Besides, they had a long waiting time."

"Britta, I am not sure. Maybe we should reconsider it."

Britta opened the car door for her mother, then she walked to the other side to get in herself. The old mother was silent. They drove home without speaking a word.

The move to the old people's home

Her room resembled a furniture warehouse, everywhere there were packed cartons. Just now Mrs. Pein brought some pots and pans and tried to stow them away in one of the open boxes. Then she gave up, for it crossed her mind that she did not need to cook anymore.

"And what about this?" Jan pointed to the teddy.

"It has to come as well." Jan pressed the big teddy in the box.

"Jan, you will come to visit me, will you?"

"Sure. Sure, I come."

"As often as you can?"

"As often as you want me to."

"Jan, I would much more like to stay, but for my daughter's sake. What time is it? Wait, I will see. Oh, a clock - I don't have a clock, best would be the big one. The tick-tock, you know? I always loved listening to the tick-tock. That's so calming. If it's quiet outside, you can hear the tick-tock of the clock."

Jan took the clock from the wall and wrapped it in newspaper. For a moment Esther Pein straightened herself and looked around bewildered.

"I don't know, Jan, maybe the clock is not such good idea."

Jan unpacked the clock again and brought it back where it was before, right beside the window.

"I would like to take everything. Or better even, unpack everything. You will come, will you?"

"As often as you want me."

"Thanks, Jan. That's good. Then every day I have something to look forward to. There won't be many to visit me. My daughter, but she is away. And six months. Six months, Jan, that's a long time."

Jan wiped the sweat from his forehead.

"How many boxes do we have?" asked Mrs. Pein and started to count. "Six and the black suitcase. If I think how small the room is, I am not sure where to put everything."

"What about the rocking chair? You wanted to take it along."

"I would love to, but they don't allow it. You should have seen the one in the room. I am not sure, if I would like to sit down. If you ask me, it did not look inviting. But to take this chair along? I don't know. I don't dare. No, Jan, I believe, this would not be good. The lady would not like it. And you don't want to make her your enemy. She is such a person, Jan. Not an easy one, believe me."

Jan thought for a while. "If the chair is there, then it is there."

"You think so?"

Jan shrugged his shoulders. "Don't know. Maybe later? If you want it later, you can let me know."

"What would I do without you, Jan!"

Mrs. Pein stood in front of the piano. Her finger softly moved across the keys. "I will miss it. Six months is a long time."

Eleven sharp a car honked.

"That is Britta."

The door bell rang and two men in blue working clothes appeared at the entrance. The one had a tiny red moustache.

"Mrs. Pein?"

"Come in."

The man with the beard nearly hit the beam in the entrance hall. He briefly looked around.

"All that?"

"These boxes and the suitcase. Wait, one box is not filled yet."

"Then let's start!" the man with the beard said and heaved the first box on his shoulders and left the room. The other man followed immediately after him with the second box. Mrs. Pein went to the bath room and came back with a chamber pot and quickly stowed it in the open box.

"That's it?"

Mrs. Pein nodded. Jan closed the box with a tape.

The telephone rang. It was Britta. She wanted to tell her mother that she was driving directly to the home without stopping at her apartment. There she wanted to wait for her mother.

Mrs. Pein looked around. Now the room seemed to be empty, even though all the furniture was still standing. In that moment she saw the bird cage.

"Hansi, I had nearly forgotten you! Jan, please, do help me!"

Jan took the bird cage from the wall. The canary fluttered anxiously up and down and hit the metal bars of the cage.

"It is afraid and does not know what is going on. Poor little thing!"

Jan held the cage in his hand, not knowing what to do.

"Maybe he will calm down, if I darken the cage. I will put a cloth on top." Mrs. Pein hurried to take the table cloth and put it over the cage.

"Don't be afraid, little friend, I am with you. Nothing will happen to you, I assure you! - Oh, the flowers, Jan, the flowers!"

"Did your daughter not say Miss Wild would take care of those?"

"That's correct, I forgot. But perhaps the cyclamen, Jan. This cyclamen I could take along. I have not seen a single flower there. Can you imagine a room without any flowers?"

Jan could not imagine.

"The cyclamen should come along." She went to the window sill to get the flower pot.

"What else?" Jan was still holding the bird cage.

"Nothing at the moment. Maybe later on. How is it, Jan, if something else comes to my mind, can I tell you? But how can I reach you? So far it was so easy, I could just come over. You don't have a telephone."

"You write down everything and when I come, you can give me the list."

The men just carried the last box out of the room.

My coat. I should not forget my coat!" Mrs. Pein went to the wardrobe, took the coat and put the hat on.

"Oh, the slippers! These I would need!" She gave Jan the flower pot, clamped the slippers under her right arm and once more looked around.

"Jan, the lamp stand! The lamp stand has to come along. I have seen what kind of light they have! Only a naked bulb underneath the ceiling, can you imagine?"

Again, Jan could not imagine. He shook his head.

"Only one little bulb at the ceiling, not even a lamp stand!"

"Won't you then take the night lamp from the night table with you along as well?"

Mrs. Pein thought for a while. "This would be nice too. And I would need a light beside my bed any way, but how?"

Jan put the bird cage on the floor and fetched the lamp stand. For a moment he was thinking. Then he took the flower pot in his left hand, the lamp stand in his right, hurried down the steps and came back with empty hands to get the bird cage. In the meantime Mrs. Pein found the umbrella. The men were waiting inside the car already. When one of the men saw the old woman, he jumped out of the car to open the door. Jan helped Mrs. Pein to go into the car and gave her the walking stick.

"You are coming, are you?" she asked with a trembling voice.

"I could come along with you right away," Jan said.

Mrs. Pein's face brightened for a moment, then it darkened again, "But how would you go back later on?"

"I will find a way."

"Britta could take you!"

Jan got in.

"Oh, I forgot to close the door!"

Jan got out to close the door. He pressed himself on the back seat between bird cage and lamp stand and flowerpot and asked, "Do you have the key?"

Mrs. Pein searched her pocket and said frightened, "I left my bag in the room on the piano!" She hesitated, then she said, "It doesn't matter. Britta has a spare key."

The car moved. It started to snow.

The first day in the retirement home

It was evening. Esther Pein was sitting on the edge of the bed and thought what she should do first. Britta together with Jan had helped to unpack the boxes and for most of the stuff they could find a space. But there were still things that absolutely did not find any room. Three boxes Britta already took home. The bird cage stood on the wardrobe. The little canary was sitting confused on the upper stake and was silent.

The gong called for supper. Mrs. Pein was not hungry at all. She looked at the clock. It was four thirty. Outside it was already dark. It was still snowing. The wind whirled the flakes against the window. The lights from passing cars were reflected from the white snow. Snowflakes were dancing in the headlights of the cars. Right now a snowplough passed. The wet snow swirled to all sides and mounted on the footpath. Esther Pein closed the curtain. There was a knock at the door. Before Mrs. Pein could call "come-in" the door was opened. Is was the lady with the bonnet.

"Time for supper."

"Are you a nurse? What shall I call you?"

"Sister Erika," she answered.

Mrs. Pein took her coat, which was still laying on the bed.

"You don't need it. The dining hall is within the house. First floor, left from the entrance."

Of course, now she remembered. "I am coming later."

The nurse left the room.

"What would happen if I don't come?" Esther Pein thought. But she could find this out another time. Now she was curious and wanted to get to know the other house guests.

When she arrived at the first floor everything seemed deserted. The hall way was sparsely lit. Behind the big glass door she could hear the clacking of the cutlery on porcelain. She opened the glass door and realized that they all were already seated and had started to eat. The nurse sat at the head of the table, that linked together the long tables at each side. For a moment Mrs. Pein was wondering what to do. She felt uncomfortable.

"We have a new house guest, Esther Pein," the nurse said. That was all. No welcome, just the fact. The old people briefly looked up and immediately continued to eat. One could hear nothing but the clacking of the cutlery. Young helpers brought plates with cold cuts and cheese. Others were serving tea. The air was filled with the smell of cabbage.

Mrs. Pein was still standing, not knowing what to do and where to turn.

"Esther Pein?" asked one of the young ladies, pointing to an empty chair. "Here."

Esther Pein sat down. She took the serviette. There was her name, and yet, it was not her name, because here the name was written with an "a". Mrs. Pein signalled the girl and pointed to the name: "Not with an "a" but an "e"!"

The girl looked bewildered and started to pour out the tea.

"Pein with an "e", Mrs. Pein said again.

The girl shook the shoulders, "then change it."

"I don't have a pen."

The young girl was already at the neighbouring place, "as if this would make a difference," Mrs. Pein heard her grumble.

Esther Pein turned to her neighbour. "Good evening. I am Esther Pein."

"Hi, can I have the sausage platter?"

Mrs. Pein reached out for the platter.

"Oh, there is still more coming, for a special occasion," the woman said in an ironic tone. One of the girls put a bowl with a yellow greyish mash on the table, nobody could identify. Then she

47

brought a second bowl with some sort of a cabbage in a sauce. The woman pushed the platter away to reach out for the bowl and started to put something on her plate. Then she poked it with her fork.

"Cooked far too long. All the vitamins are dead by now. No wonder that I get rheumatism." The woman showed Esther Pein her crippled fingers. "But I tell you, all they want is our money. Look what we get for that!" In spite of that she started to shovel the mash into her mouth, and continued to talk with food in her mouth. "You will find out about this place pretty soon, believe me."

"How long have you lived here?"

"If you ask me, far too long."

Esther Pein took a slice of bread. Cold cuts were no longer available. She took some cheese and started to spread it on the bread. Should I ask to bring some more? she wondered. But when nobody said anything, she gave up. She felt relieved when finally the bell rang and the meal was ended.

The old people were pushing to get out. Nobody greeted her. Only at the elevator one old lady asked: "You are new here?"

"Yes, I am. My name is Esther Pein. And what about you?"

"Magda Wise."

"Have you been here long?"

"Depending."

The elevator stopped. Magda Wise left and Esther Pein realized they were neighbours.

Hardly had Esther Pein opened her door when loud music met her from the neighbour's room. The canary was still sitting without moving at the same spot. It had not eaten anything yet.

Have patience, little friend, until I've found a better place."

She started to clean up the things from her bed and put one piece after the other into the wardrobe. She opened the second door of the wardrobe and realized that it was already taken. Her room mate was not here yet. Esther Pein put the light stand on the little table beside her bed. A warm light fell on her bed sheet. The huge television set of the neighbouring room started to bother her.

"This would be the right place for the floor lamp." she told herself and started to move the television, but it was too heavy. She waited and put the floor lamp behind the door but moved it again when she realized that then the door would damage the lamp shade. This time the lamp ended directly behind the television.

"Now listen, you are behaving as if this room would belong only to you!"

Ester Pein startled and gazed into the frozen face of a stout woman. The grey hair were hanging in long strains from her head, which gave her an appearance of someone uncared for. In the thick glasses mirrored the light of the bulb, that was fixed to the ceiling. She stepped to the television and turned it on and started to undress herself. The television rumbled. Esther Pein waited to see if she would turn down the level, but apparently that's what her neighbour liked.

"I am Esther Pein," she introduced herself.

"Baumgarten, Lisa Baumgarten."

"Nice to meet you."

"Nice to meet me? You don't know me yet. There is nothing nice around here, nothing, believe me."

Esther Pein did not say anything. She was about to take off her socks, when from the wardrobe she heard a tiny chirp.

"What's that?" Lisa Baumgarten asked.

"A canary."

"I can see that! Don't you know that we are not allowed to keep an animal?"

"That's not a dog or a cat."

"I can see that too. Still it's forbidden."

"And why? It doesn't do any harm."

"It makes noise and dirt, that's what it does."

"It sings."

"That's bad enough."

The television was so loud that the two women started to shout at each other.

"No, I can't stand this," Esther Pein thought, "not 24 weeks. Not even one week. Maybe one night." "Can't you turn down the television?" she asked her neighbour.

"Then I can't hear."

On the screen you could just see how two women undressed themselves and started to touch each other.

49

"But I don't like this program!"

"That's too bad. But at eight o'clock I am turning it off anyway, at eight I am going to sleep."

"At eight o'clock? That early?"

"That's what my daughter said too."

Esther Pein looked at her watch. She was not tired yet.

Eight o'clock sharp the television was switched off. Esther Pein relaxed.

"It bothers me when there is light."

"But I can't sleep that early."

"Don't care, but I need my sleep."

Esther thought about what she should do. Even one night would be too much. "I can't cope with that," she thought. She sat on her bed and started to cry. She longed for her own apartment. If only Jan would be here. But Jan was not here.

"You can go in the lounge," she heard the voice of Miss Baumgarten.

"But why? This is my room as well."

"I will sleep and the light bothers me, that's why!"

Esther Pein put the remaining things from her bed and was wondering what to do with the rest of the boxes. She was about to undress herself, when she heard the snoring of her neighbour.

From the next room she could still hear the music. "Maybe I should say something. But on my first day?" The rhythm was constantly the same. Esther realized that her feet started to hammer the beat. "Pein, here is something to learn, that's for sure," she talked to herself. "Now you are that old already and still can learn something new. But what?"

She glimpsed to her neighbour. Her glasses were on the little night table beside a box of pills. In a glass dentures were covered with water.

"Oh God, sometimes it's not easy to love my neighbour. Don't you think this is a bit too much to ask? I never thought about it. But a bit of tact would not be too difficult to expect? I don't expect much, just a little. But this my neighbour - she did not have any training as a child."

From the other room she could hear the coloratura soprano. She knew the opera. It was a part from Othello by Verdi.

"In this house there is no peace. Only now I realise how spoiled I was. And I had taken everything for granted. Is that what I have to learn? Then I am ready to learn, but please in a crash course! Not six months! This I can tell you, I can't. No, I can't - and I don't want to!"

Determined she left the room and knocked at her neighbour's door. Nobody answered. She knocked again, then she opened slowly the door. Magda Wise sat in her pyjama in a chair in front of the television and looked at her in surprise.

"What happened?"

"Could you please turn the television down?"

"But then I can't hear."

"But it bothers me." Esther Pein realized that her heart hammered wildly.

"You don't like music? You don't know what you are missing!"

I do like music, but I prefer to decide for myself what kind of music and when I listen to it."

Magda Wise was totally enthralled by the play. "To be honest, it's more or less the same all the time, but still better than what we have here. I need something to kill the time."

Magda Wise did not turn down the television. Esther Pein looked around secretly. The room indeed resembled her own room exactly. The same furniture, only the colour of the sofa was different. Also there was only one bed at the wall instead of two.

"Since you are here already, you may sit down just as well."

Esther Pein sat down. Now Magda Wise looked at her. "Could it be that we met before? You remind me somehow of somebody I knew."

She shrugged her shoulders, "perhaps I am wrong. Old people always look the same more or less." She laughed. Her teeth were as grey as her hair.

"I wanted to be an opera singer myself when I was young. But my parents didn't want me to. A girl has to be at home to take care of her family and the kids. You should say this to a young girl today! My daughter would have laughed at me!"

"How old is your daughter?"

"Well, a couple of years ago we celebrated her fiftieth, only in a small circle of friends. She does not want anybody to know how old she is. That too is something I don't understand. I am proud about my age. I am 85, I tell everybody, if they want to hear it or not. But most of the time they want to hear and are surprised. "I would never have guessed that," they tell me then, as if this would be something special. The young people today are funny."

"Birthdays in my village were always something special, like a village event," Esther Pein remembered. "Everybody knew how old everybody was."

"At our place this was different. We lived in a huge estate. I didn't even know who lived beside us. Everybody wanted to be private. Nothing to share. But it's the same here. Nobody knows who lives in the next room."

Esther Pein got up. Magda Wise laughed. "Too excited? Not good for the night?"

"Maybe you should get a hearing aid?"

"What did you say?"

If the dear neighbour doesn't like it

Somehow she managed to survive the first night. When she woke up the next morning, the world did not seem so bad any more. The sun managed to peek through a gap in the curtain. Esther Pein folded back the bed cover and looked around. She was alone in the room. She had not even heard when Miss Baumgarten left the room. She opened the window and took a deep breath. In the distance she could see a mountain range. The sun glittered on the white cap.

Somehow she felt uprooted. She thought about what to do next. "Best would be to explore the area. I have to know where I am," she told herself.

She was about to leave the house when she was startled. Close to the bench at the entrance there she saw a small figure of an old woman in a wheelchair. The woman seemed to be asleep. The head was bent forward on her chest, her hands rested in her lap. Esther Pein stepped beside her.

"Can I do something for you?"

The old woman in the wheelchair raised her head and smiled. "I am waiting for my son. He will be here any moment. It's good to have a son, don't you think so too? Do you have a son?"

"I have a daughter. She is in the States."

"Oh."

"But just for a couple of weeks," she added quickly.

"To have somebody, that makes all the difference."

"Yes," Esther Pein said.

"I saw you yesterday but did not have a chance to talk to you. I liked it what you said about your name. Pein without the a. That really impressed me. When I am back, please come and visit me. Room 106."

"106" Esther Pein repeated. "And what is your name?"

"Sorry, I have not even introduced myself. Angelica Raiman. There is my son!"

A man about 40 dressed in a thick dark blue parka hastened to come closer. A cold wind blew from the entrance. He bent down to his mother and kissed her on the forehead. He nodded briefly towards Mrs. Pein.

"This is Esther Pein," Angelica Raiman introduced her, "Pein without an a."

He looked somehow bewildered and did not seem to understand.

"Raiman," he said, looking at Esther Pein. And then to his mother,

"Let's go!" Without waiting for an answer he grabbed the wheelchair and pushed his mother to the exit. She turned once more and said: "Room 106, don't forget! I am back Sunday evening after supper."

"I promise, I'll be there!" She was wondering why the day looked so much brighter. "Angelica Raiman," she repeated not to forget the name.

Esther Pein looked at the sky. Maybe it would be better to take the umbrella along and went back to fetch it. She was about to open the door of her room when she stepped back in surprise. How could it be that the bird cage was standing in the hallway? She nearly fell over it. Carefully she lifted the cage up and took it back to the room. Miss Baumgarten was sitting in the chair, fast asleep. The television was still playing. Esther Pein put the bird cage on a chair and shut off the television. At that moment Miss Baumgarten opened her eyes and without saying a word turned the television on again.

"But you don't watch it," Esther Pein protested.

"The sound calms me down."

"Listen, neighbour, can't we come up with an agreement?"

"What kind of agreement do you mean? If it bothers you then go somewhere else."

"And what about the bird cage? Can you explain how this cage came into the hall way?"

"The bird makes me crazy. This hobbling from one stake to the next, and besides, it's forbidden to keep animals."

At that moment the nurse entered the room with the mail. She handed Esther Pein a postcard, then she saw the bird cage.

"How on earth did this come here?" she asked with a stern voice.

"That's mine. That is a canary."

"Don't you know that it is forbidden to bring animals inside the house? Animals are the cause of infections."

"My Hansi won't bring any sickness in here."

The face of the nurse turned red. "Mrs. Pein this goes too far. I have to report this to the management."

"Then go ahead and do it." Esther Pein realized that she too turned red. She was fuming.

The nurse left and closed the door behind her.

"I told you," Miss Baumgarten said triumphantly.

Esther Pein took the chair that was standing beside her bed in front of the wardrobe, then reached for the cage and mounted

54

carefully on the chair to place the cage on the wardrobe where it was before.

"You lost your voice, didn't you, little friend? As long as we have been here you have not sung once. Just wait, in a couple of days we will move into a one bedroom. Then we can talk with each other."

A couple of minutes had passed when there was a knock at the door and again before waiting for an answer, the door was opened and the manager appeared. She looked around but could not see what she was looking for.

"I heard something about a queer bird?"

"I would not call it that," Esther Pein said with a smile.

"Do you have a bird or not?"

"If you are talking about the canary, yes I do have a bird. There he is."

"I am sorry to tell you that he can't stay in the house."

"And why not, if I may ask?"

"That is against the rules."

"And who made those rules?"

"What do you mean?"

"I mean, this is a regulation we can talk about."

"There is nothing to talk about. I hope, you understand."

Mrs. Liebreich turned to leave the room.

"Just a moment, Mrs. Liebreich, I want to talk to you."

"I tell you right here, I won't change my mind."

"Then I can tell you, that this is not the right place for me to be."

Esther Pein could hardly subdue her anger. She trembled that badly that she had to sit down. She could not contain her tears any longer and wiped her eyes.

"Now Britta is on her way, somewhere high up in the air and I can't go home, I am trapped," she thought. "If only I would have stayed home!"

At exactly 2:30 Jan stood in front of the door. Esther Pein embraced him so wildly, that his cap fell from his head. He looked bewildered and did not know what happened. He got his cap from the floor and looked at Esther Pein. Then he smiled sheepishly and looked at Miss Baumgarten, but she did not even realize it. She was sleeping again.

"How did you manage to come in? Who let you in?"

"The door was open, so I just went through. I knew where you were anyway," he said in a low voice not to awaken the sleeping lady.

Esther Pein shoved him excitingly out of the room. She looked around and then said in a whisper: "Let's go to the lounge. I can't talk here." She just had closed the door, when she sighed and said, "Jan, I think, I won't make it here. It would be best if I returned home with you. They are not human. Every body tries to make life as miserable as possible." Their steps sounded hollow on the carpet. "I can't understand, why people can be so mean to each other. And it could be so nice. But everybody tries to put stones in the way."

"Is it that bad?"

"Even worse than you can imagine. I have never seen something like that. They are treating us as - - as- - "

Jan nodded.

"I have the impression, they are poisoning us. It's strange, a rotten apple affects a healthy one, but I never have experienced that a healthy apple can change a rotten one so you could eat it."

"Maybe they are afraid. Like animals when they are afraid."

"Afraid? For what?"

"For life? I don't know. Of each other?"

"Maybe. Yes, maybe you are right. Only then they feel strong. They feel strong as long as they are against something or somebody."

She turned into another hall way. Jan was at her side. "Are they all the same?"

Esther Pein thought for a while. Suddenly the face of the lady in the wheelchair appeared in front of her eyes. "Maybe not everybody. Maybe there is one exception."

They had reached the lounge. Esther Pein opened the door and let Jan enter first. They were on their own. The large window was closed. Esther Pein tried to open it, but it would not open. So she gave up. Then Jan tried.

"You can't open the window," he said. Only the little one above. Jan opened the little window. Immediately cold snow flakes came in. So he closed it again.

"And you came in spite of this weather!"

"I promised to."

"Did you come by bus?"

"My brother Charles took me. He had something to do in town. At 5 he will pick me up again."

"That early?" she asked disappointed. "You know what? If this would be a home, I mean a real home, then I would invite both of you for supper. But this is not possible. Regrettably it would not be possible."

Jan did not seem to listen.

"It is nice here," he said and looked around. "There is even a fire place and a piano."

"A piano?" Esther Pein was surprised that she had not seen that before. She opened the cover and tried a few tunes. A hollow, rattling noise, without any melody. She closed the cover. "The piano fits this house. Out of tune."

Jan did not hear what Esther Pein said, he looked at the huge picture on the wall and said, "We had such a picture at home in our living room. I still remember. The shepherd leading his sheep back home at sunset. When I was a boy I looked at this picture often and wished I was a shepherd. The atmosphere. Such peace. Without time."

Esther Pein looked at the picture, she had to admit she had never seen it before. She looked around to find the best spot to sit down.

"Maybe over there in the niche."

There were two chairs made of wicker with some cushions. Jan pulled the chair and waited for Esther Pein to sit down, then he too sat down, took the cap from his head and started to play with it. He looked down and did not say a word.

"I have to admit I did not think it would be this bad," Esther Pein said. "Somehow I thought I would get used to it, but this does not look like it will ever happen. What would you do if your dear neighbour does not want to live in peace? But look at these people.

Are they happy? Are they happy?" she asked again. Without waiting for an answer she continued: "There is no laughter. No humour. No joy."

"But you only came here yesterday."

"Was is yesterday? Really? Are you sure?"

He nodded.

"I thought it was before that."

"Yesterday in the afternoon you moved in. That was Wednesday. Today is Thursday."

"You are right. I thought it was last week."

"Did you not say you could soon move into a one bed room?"

"That's what they promised. But I am not even sure, if I want to. Do you know that the bird cage was standing in front of my door this morning? Just so, without talking with me. This is unheard of."

"Did you talk with the mother of the home?"

"Mother?" she asked in a ironic tone.

Jan looked at her. "There are good mothers, and there are bad ones."

"You are right. And this one belongs to the bad sort. Sorry to say. I tried to talk to her. There is nothing. She has a heart of stone."

"This morning Helena came to your door. She was about to turn, when I saw her. I invited her in, but she ran away."

"Did she say anything?"

"She did not say anything."

"If only I knew where she lives. Listen Jan, could you find out where she lives?"

"I don't know. It would be a bit difficult."

"I understand. Do you know where the kindergarten is?"

Jan nodded.

"How about I write a few lines and give you the letter?"

"Can she read?"

"Not she, but her mother can. I have to explain why I did not come."

"I can deliver the letter." He took a small parcel out of his jacket. "I nearly forgot. It's for you."

"For me?" Esther Pein took the neatly wrapped parcel and started to open the red ribbon.

"How nice this is packaged!"

Jan's face brightened. "I bought it this morning before I came here."

"In the village store?"

"Yes. Martha says hello."

"Then she knows I am here?"

"I told her."

Esther opened the little parcel and hold up a flowery mug. "How beautiful, Jan!" She looked around as if looking for something. Then she got up. "You know what, Jan? The two of us will have a cup of coffee. Over there at the desk is a coffee maker and some plastic cups and some coffee. At least we can have a cup of coffee. There even are some sweets."

"I brought something else," Jan said and took from his pocket a foam box. "From our store."

Esther recognised the cake. She took the plastic cups and poured hot water on top of the instant coffee. "It doesn't taste like at home, but it will do." Then she put the two cups on a small tray and carried it to the little table. Jan sprang up to help her with the tray. His cap fell to the ground. He took it, put it on his chair, then he helped Esther Pein to carry the tray to the table. She trembled so badly that she spilled some of the coffee.

"Don't worry, I'll fix it," Jan said and took his handkerchief and wiped the table.

"It's a long time since we had coffee together, isn't it?"

"Yes indeed. You know, when I see you, I feel better already. But the thing with the cage, this I don't understand. I don't know what to do."

"I could take it back home with me," Jan suggested.

"In that weather? The little one would freeze to death."

"But I told you, my brother will come and pick me up."

Esther Pein did not say anything.

"He could stay with me in the workshop."

She did not listen. "I can't understand, why they don't allow it. The little bird does not do any harm to anybody."

"It's not the same, since you are gone," Jan said.

"Thanks, Jan. I miss you too. I thought a lot last night. Here everybody is bored just waiting for the next meal. They only talk about food and illness. As if there is nothing else to talk about. And of course the television. The whole day. What a life!"

Esther Pein took a piece of cake. "It tastes like home."

"There is not much left in our store," Jan said.

In the hall way one could hear muffled voices. The door was open but closed again.

"You know what I miss here most? A joyful laughter. Children's voices. If Helena would be here... I mean, not just for a visit. Please remind me to write a few lines before you leave."

"Six months, you said?"

"About. But if I can make it, I am not sure."

"Mrs. Pein I have to run a few errands before going home. In this neighbourhood there is a hobby store. I will look around. Is it all right with you if I come back in a couple of minutes?"

"You want to leave already?"

"I am not sure when the stores are closing. I need some tools and wanted to see if I can find them here."

Esther Pein thought for a moment. "If the weather would be nice, I would have loved to come with you, for I haven't been to the neighbourhood at all. Is it far?"

"Just a couple of blocks. But the street is slippery."

"You are coming back again?"

"It won't take long."

"Maybe I should talk again with Mrs. Liebreich. If I know you are coming back, I would dare."

Jan put his cap on. They both went to the entrance door. Jan asked in a whisper; "Is the front door always locked?"

"Yes. But you can ring the bell. Until four somebody is always in the office. And I am here anyway and will wait for you."

The heavy entrance door closed automatically.

Esther Pein turned to the office. Behind the glass she could see the nurse, who looked up briefly but soon busied herself with some paper work. Esther Pein cleared her throat.

"Excuse me!" No reaction. "Excuse me! Can I talk to Mrs. Liebreich?" she asked through the window.

"She is busy with a visitor," the nurse said without looking up.

Esther Pein opened the door and stepped inside the office. "I'll wait here," she said firmly.

The nurse turned red but did not say anything. In the very moment the door to the bureau was opened and a young lady left. Esther Pein looked briefly at the nurse and read the sign in bold letters *MANAGER. DO NOT DISTURB*! She knocked at the door and opened it before somebody invited her in. "That's what they are doing all the time," she thought.

Mrs. Liebreich looked up in surprise. Esther Pein took a deep breath and said, "Excuse me, that I disturb you, but I would like to talk to you."

"What about?"

"I would like to keep the canary, otherwise I can't stay."

"I thought this matter was closed. We can't make any exception. I told you very clearly. That's the rule."

Esther Pein sat down on the black leather chair and felt uncomfortable. Her voice trembled. "Some houses have large aquariums. I heard this should have a calming effect on the people." Esther Pein looked around. No, there was not a sign of life around here. On the floor a large pot with artificial flowers.

"And who will do the cleanup?" asked Mrs. Liebreich and scribbled some numbers on a piece of paper. "Such an aquarium is a lot of work. To look at it is not enough. An aquarium needs constant care." She put the pen aside and looked at Esther Pein. " The water has to be changed regularly, the fish need food, and what if there is a sickness? This is not so easy."

"Old people need life around them. They need something they can take over responsibility for."

"They want their peace, that's all!" Mrs. Liebreich again scribbled something on a paper and took the receiver.

"We are not in the cemetery yet, Mrs. Liebreich. This house is a prison!"

Mrs. Liebreich dialled, but immediately put the receiver back. "Do you want to insult me?" she asked with a sharp voice.

"Even prisoners - nowadays at least in this country - have certain rights. But here?" Mrs. Pein was startled. Never before she had spoken to somebody else in that way. Her heart pounded wildly. She stroked her long skirt and waited. She had made up her mind not to leave until this matter was settled. Her hands became clammy, her mouth dry. She had been here only one day and already she wanted to change something that always worked. She realized that all that was far too early, but she was desperate. Something had to be done. And Britta was not there, she thought again. I can't go back.

"If I permit you today to keep the bird, then somebody else comes tomorrow and wants to keep their cat, and still somebody else his dog. Then we can start a zoo." Mrs. Liebreich again took the receiver and dialled. Still the busy signal. She put the receiver back. Mrs. Pein took a deep breath.

"I heard that in Holland people can bring their pets along when they have to go to a home."

"We are not in Holland. I told you, here there are no animals allowed."

Mrs. Pein took another deep breath and dared a new attempt. "Don't you think it could be a help for somebody to have something around they could love? Especially when they feel lonely. Something familiar, a living being with whom they could talk."

"That's where we come in."

"Is that so?" "But what if nobody dares to talk to you?" but this she did not say aloud. Mrs. Pein was silent.

"Something else?" Mrs. Liebreich used all her strength to be friendly.

"Yes. When I was at home on my own, I often sat in my chair listening to the song of this little bird. It was a heavenly voice. And then I talked to him, and I had the feeling this little creature understands. We belonged together. The little bird and I. I can't send him back. I just can't. We belong together, the little bird and I. I can't send him back. He would not survive."

Mrs. Liebreich didn't say anything. She glared in front of her.

"Maybe I could put the cage in the lounge, then others could see him as well."

Mrs. Liebreich still was silent.

"I promise, I will take care of it. I will clean up as I always did at home."

Mrs. Liebreich was silent.

"You know if you are getting old you have to say good-bye to many things. It is even more important to have something familiar around."

"O.K. Do what you want. But if somebody complains the bird has to go."

Mrs. Pein thought she did not hear right. To be sure, she asked: "I can keep it?"

"If you want it so desperately, I don't care."

Mrs. Pein stretched. She did not know what to say. She could have embraced her, but she did not want to overreact, for in her eyes this was the normal thing to do. But she could see that much: the hard skin got a tiny crack. There was hope.

"Thanks." She said and got up.

Mrs. Liebreich took the receiver again and dialled. Mrs. Pein left the office and closed the door carefully not to make any noise.

She went back into her room. Miss Baumgarten was not there. She pushed the chair in front of the wardrobe and climbed carefully on the chair. Then she opened the door so she had something to hold onto in order not to lose the balance. She reached out with her left to get the cage, while still holding on with her right hand to the door. She realized how she trembled. The canary fluttered anxiously up and down. Inch by inch she lowered the cage and put it on her bed. Then she stepped down herself. She took a deep breath and had to sit down first. Then she took out of the drawer of the night table the writing pad, clamped it under her left arm, took the cage and carried it to the lounge. The writing utensils she put on the table.

"So far so good, Hansi. What do you say now? We made it! What do you think? Where do you want to be? Here? Or rather there?" she asked and carried the cage to the long low bookcase, that was standing between the windows.

"Here you are protected and you can see what is going on. And as soon as I have my own room, you can come to me to be close to me again. As soon as there is a room available, believe me! Until then you can wait here for me. Nobody will say a word, and I will come as often as possible and take care of you as always. I do hope, you will sing again? For me?"

The little bird crouched in the corner and trembled.

"Don't be afraid, Hansi, don't take that to heart. Sometimes everything looks so bleak but it is only half as bad as we think."

She looked outside to the street. It had stopped snowing. Just now the light of the street lights were lit. The snow started to glow.

"There comes Jan! You remember Jan? Wait, I will be back in a second!"

She came just in time to open the door for Jan. He shook the wet snow from his jacket and took the cap off.

"Can you imagine, Jan, she has allowed it. I can keep Hansi. I still can't believe it! Come in. Did you find what you were looking for?"

"Yes."

They had reached the lounge. "He did not sing once. It's the atmosphere, Jan, everything is so dark. This little thing feels it. How should an old person be happy?"

"I don't know what to say," said Jan.

Mrs. Pein laughed. It was the first time that she laughed since she came here. "Of course not, what should you say? But maybe there is a meaning behind why I am here. I don't know yet. It's a kind of culture shock. Yes, indeed a culture shock, that what it is."

"Culture shock? What do you mean by that?" Jan asked and took off his wet jacket and hung it over the chair.

"You know, if somebody moves to a different culture he suffers such an emotional stage that he can't understand himself. Many get depressed and lose all interest. They don't have any strength left to live. Everything looks bleak and without any hope. I think this is similar. It's a strange country I am in right now. They all speak a different language."

"Why do they speak a different language? Are they not from here?"

"I mean the language of the heart, Jan. When we both look at each other, we do understand. But these people here - I just can't understand them. I am afraid of them."

"Then come back with me again. We can take you with us."

"It's good to know that you are there, but Britta would be worried."

"She does not need to know."

"She promised to call here. And when she calls and knows that I left, she would return home immediately. And then I could not forgive myself. I don't want her to plan her life around me."

"Did you know that two streets from here the Christmas market is coming?"

"No, I did not know."

"My brother Charles has a booth there as well. It looks very nice. You won't believe what you can buy there!"

Esther Pein realized that her cheeks started to glow. "It's the coffee, Jan, the coffee starts to work."

"You should come and have a look. In the evening it must be especially pretty with all the lights. Unfortunately I have to go back soon. But perhaps when I come back next time."

"The letter, Jan, I shouldn't forget the letter. Please, wait."

Esther Pein went to the table, sat down on the chair and wrote a couple of lines, then she took the envelope, put the letter inside and sealed it. Then she wrote in large letters: TO HELENA VENICETTI. She got up and handed Jan the letter.

"Thanks, Jan. Don't forget. And thanks for coming. I can't tell you how much that meant for me."

The child and the shadow

When Jan left it was lonely again. Before she entered her room, she waited outside and listened. Could it be that she was afraid to go in?

"What would she come up with this time?" Mrs. Pein was wondering. "Surely she would have something she doesn't like. If only I could be on my own, close the door, not seeing anybody."

She opened the door. Miss Baumgarten was busy packing her things. Now she went to the wardrobe to take her clothes out.

"Do you want to travel?" Mrs. Pein asked full of hope.

"Travel sounds good. I have to go to the hospital for some examinations."

"Are you sick?"

"Breast cancer."

"I am sorry to hear. I had no idea."

Miss Baumgarten did not say a word. The television played.

"Can I do something for you?"

"It's not necessary."

"Do you have children?"

"One daughter in Australia." She stopped talking and took her suitcase out of the storage room. "I want to apologise about the bird. I am sorry."

"We found a place for it."

"You still have it?"

"The cage is in the lounge. I do hope he will sing again soon."

"I'm sure he will as soon as he gets used to this new surrounding. I too once had such a bird. It's long ago. Our cat ate it." Miss Baumgarten continued to pack.

"How long have you lived here?"

"Two years. And if you ask me, two years too long. But I didn't know where to go. To go to my daughter's wasn't possible. And who will go to Australia! She could have waited until I am under the ground."

"That doesn't sound hopeful."

"Am I not right?"

"Don't you have any relatives here?"

"Fortunately not."

"What does that mean?"

"If you knew them, you would understand." Then she continued, "I hate hospitals. You are not allowed to be dressed in your own clothes. You get a kind of hospital robe, a blueish rag with some strips to close at the back. And besides, far too short. Do you know what they said when I complained? We are not on a fashion show! As soon as you go there, you have to give up your humanity together with all your valuables. Then you don't count any more. Am I in a KZ, a concentration camp? Valuables and human nature were taken from you. From then on you are a number. Nothing else. They don't care."

"They are not all the same."

"Listen, don't say that. Everything is money. Even cutting toenails. Everything. There is nothing for nothing. Everything is money." Miss Baumgarten closed the suitcase. "What did I get from life? Work and problems "

"Is there nothing nice you have experienced?"

"Me? No. Or do you think war is something nice? And what followed after the war? No, there is nothing nice about it. I once was engaged. We wanted to marry. But he died before the child was born. So I never married."

Esther Pein felt helpless. She did not dare to ask more questions, but she did not want to tell about her own life either. And to say something to encourage her - this would call for an ugly reaction. She fell silent. The television was still going on. Esther Pein undressed herself and got ready for bed.

"That was a good idea with the lamp. I got used to the darkness. But now I know the difference."

"I am glad that it helped you as well. Sometimes there are those little things that make a difference in our lives."

"That's true, but these people won't think that way."

Esther Pein took a book from the bookcase and flipped through the pages. Then she found one story.

"Shall I read something to you?"

"If it's not too long."

"A short story."

Miss Baumgarten turned off the television. For a moment it was very quiet in the room. Esther Pein sat in the bed and stuck the pillow behind her back, took her glasses from the night table and put them on.

"Shall I?"

"I am waiting."

"The child and the shadow. It's a fairy tale," Esther Pein explained. Then she read:

The child was standing at the lake shore. The sun was playing with the soft waves and strew silvery sparks. The wind moved softly through the high reed blades, shadows danced over the water. A waterfowl got up with heavy flapping and soared over the soft trembling surface of the water, then it disappeared and pulled his shadow after him. At the distant shore the fir trees stretched, casting dark shadows over the sea so that their crown drew pointed figures on the water surface. The child looked forlorn at the soft waves of the water, watching her own reflection and let the water spill through her little fingers.

This was her image and she could give this image a hundred different expressions. Then she saw again the face of her little brother in her mind. "He will die," her father had said, "Because he's already signed by the shadow of death." The child did not understand what that meant, but knew that the shadow was an enemy of life. Why did she feel so helpless? Was there nothing she could do? Really nothing? "I will kill the shadow so it can't harm my little brother," she told herself but did not know how she could kill the shadow.

From the nearby pasture she heard the neighing of a horse. The child stretched and clapped her hands. Out of the shadow of the tree came a horse and trotted leisurely towards the child. In front of the fence it halted and waited. The child greeted the horse and stroked gently along the long mane, hiding her face in the soft fur of the slender neck. The horse softly bowed its neck and remained still. Then it raised its beautiful head and pointed its ears as if listening to far away music. The child stretched out her little hands and could sense the soft lips. Then the horse shook its long mane and waited. At that very moment the child saw the shadow of the horse and startled. "You will die for you are carrying the shadow of death," the child said, "but don't be afraid, I will destroy the shadow as I will destroy the shadow of my little brother." And the child started to dig a deep hole to catch the shadow. Then it shovelled earth on top, but when she looked up she realized that the shadow escaped its grave, so she started to dig another hole, this time even deeper. And when she saw that the shadow was exactly in the hole, she hurriedly covered it with dirt as before. At that moment the horse moved and took the shadow along with it. "Wait! Don't run away!" the little girl cried in despair. "I will paint your shadow white, wait!" She hurried to the shed to fetch a bucket with white paint. When she returned the horse trotted towards the child again and stretched its long neck over the fence. Then it shook its mane as if asking, "what are you doing there, little friend?" The child took some of the paint and poured it on the sand. and the sand swallowed the paint. "I will paint the whole world white," she said to herself. But it did not take much time and the bucket was empty and the child realized with panic that the shadow grew even longer than before. She started to cry.

"Arina!" that was the voice of her father.

The child ran toward her father.

"I told you, you should not go to the lake shore on your own!"

"But I wanted to kill the shadow."

"Kill the shadow? What do you mean?"

"You told me that the shadow of death rested upon my little brother, and I did not want the shadow to kill my brother, therefore I wanted to kill the shadow."

"You can't kill the shadow. The shadow belongs to life. It's a sign of light. Only during the night we can't see the shadow, because the whole world turns into shade. But when the sun breaks through the clouds and the moon brightens the earth, then shadows grow again."

The child did not understand.

"Is the shadow not something bad?"

"It's neither good nor evil."

"What is it then?"

"It's a mystery, and a mystery you can't explain. You see the horse over there? Because it stands there and the sun is shining, it creates a shadow. You have to kill the horse to kill its shadow."

"But I don't want to kill the horse. The horse is my friend. It has not done anything bad to me."

"I know. And you are not supposed to kill the horse. The trees too have shadows. Even you and I."

The child saw shadows dancing across the meadow.

"Does all that have to die?"

69

"One day all that won't be here anymore."

"But I don't want to die."

"Life is inside of you. And this life is without any shadow, for that life within you is from God. And God is light."

"Doesn't God have any shadow?"

"God is without form and space and time."

"Is he far away?"

"He is everywhere."

"Also in the sea and on the mountains?"

"Also in the sea and on the mountains."

"And here?"

"Here too."

"Why can't I see him?"

"Can you see the wind?"

"I can hear it and see how it moves the reeds."

"Yes," her father said, "you can. You can see this world God had made."

"But why can't I see God?"

"Only with the eyes of your heart can you see him."

"Does our heart have eyes too?"

"Yes, but we have to learn how to use them."

"Is the world the shadow of God?"

"Yes, maybe. Whatever is in the way of the light casts a shadow."

"I don't understand. Did God make the shadow too?"

"Yes, child," her father said.

"I am afraid of the shadow."

"You don't need to be afraid of the shadow, Arina," her father said.

"If I am big, can I then kill the shadow?"

At that moment the sun broke through the branches and the child stepped frightened aside, because she saw that she was standing on the shadow of her father.

"You can't kill the shadow, but you can learn to read the shadow, for the shadow is talking about light."

"Can you pray that the shadow disappears?"

70

"Shall I pray that the horse is no longer there? If it is no longer there, then it would not cast any shadow."

"Does God always do what you want?"

"I pray, and if he gives what I had asked for, I say: praise be thy name."

"And if he doesn't give you?"

"If he does not give me, I say, praise be thy name. For not what he gives is important, but who he is."

"Why is my shadow that small?" asked the child.

The father took his child on his shoulders, "Can you see the large shadow? Now it's as tall as the tree. The bigger the shadow the closer we are to the source of the light. Only when we are totally absorbed by the light, we will lose our shadow."

Esther Pein put the book aside.

"That's a nice story. It reminds me of past times. I always tried to catch my shadow. He tricked me out every time. The shadow of the war caught us and wiped out one after another. I got engaged just a year before the war broke out. My fiancee never saw the child. That's life. But that was a nice story. Do you have more of those?"

"I can lend you the book so you have something to read." Esther Pein gave her the book. Miss Baumgarten took it and turned over the leaves.

"It can't hurt to have a good book, although they won't give me much time."

When Esther Pein returned the next morning from breakfast, the room was empty. At first she stopped in surprise, then she felt guilty. Maybe I was too hasty with my judgement, she thought. Maybe she is not that unapproachable as I thought in the beginning. And she decided to visit her as soon as possible in the hospital.

Mrs. Raiman

It was Sunday evening. Esther Pein calculated that Mrs. Raiman should be home by now. She made sure again that she was at the right door. No 106. She knocked softly. There was silence. She knocked again, this time louder.

"Come in!"

Esther Pein felt uncomfortable. She was somehow timid and was not used to visiting in other people's home.

"Mrs. Pein! I had hoped you would come!"

Mrs. Raiman stretched her hand out and asked Esther Pein to push the chair closer. "Then I can see better."

Esther Pein sat down on a cushioned rocker. Maybe this was her own? it flashed through her mind. The wheelchair was beside the bed. On the little table there were two crutches.

"I am still a bit out off breath," Mrs. Raiman said with a smile, "my daily gymnastic, you know?"

"Then you don't need to sit all the time in the wheelchair?"

"I try every day at least once to move only with the help of these crutches. But come, let's talk about something else. I am glad you came. Would you like a glass of wine?"

This question took her by surprise and Mrs. Pein did not know how to answer.

"Would you?" Mrs. Raiman asked again. "In that case I would ask you to get two glasses from the cupboard. And behind the curtain in a bucket you will see the bottle. My son gave it to me tonight, "for a special occasion," he said.

"To be honest, I am not a wine drinker, but today, why not?"

She got up and took the glasses and then the bottle. While passing she saw some books piled on a board. "You like to read?" Mrs. Pein pointed to the books.

"What else is there to do? We have far too much time here. That's not always a blessing. You have to keep yourself busy with something, especially if you are handicapped. In my youth I was a sports teacher - until the accident. That's years ago. Already I am talking about sickness!" She laughed. "That's like an addiction. As soon as we have the opportunity to talk, we talk about sickness. After all there are so many other things to talk about."

"I am glad that I can come," Mrs. Pein admitted. "Please tell me about this house."

Mrs. Raiman hesitated. "That's not easy. It would be best for you to find out yourself. But come, let's drink on our acquaintance."

Mrs. Pein lifted the glass. "To our acquaintance! - but please, don't make excuses. To be honest, when I came, I was about to return home at the very first moment."

Mrs. Raiman laughed. "It was different with me. When I arrived, I thought I was in paradise."

Mrs. Pein looked at her in surprise.

"You have no idea where I was before! Before that I could not do as much as I can today, I was totally dependant on help. This can be very humiliating, as you can imagine." She looked down in deep thought. "I had the feeling even the last dignity was taken from me, to be a human being. But maybe somebody first has to be helpless to be able to understand somebody else. They all were young and healthy, who were working there. I can't blame them. But it hurt. "Granma, come on, open your mouth! So, that's fine..." Mrs. Raiman laughed "Today I can laugh, but not then. The house I was in was really luxurious in comparison with this one. Nothing was missing, only humanness."

"You mean you can have that here?"

"It depends how much help you need, perhaps. I was totally helpless. But nobody had time. Besides, it was very far away for my son to visit. It was just too far to visit me every day. My son could not take it any longer and he brought me here. I have to admit, it's not all perfect, and I am sure, there are better homes around, but much depends how one reacts to a situation. For one person it's like a paradise, for the next one it can be hell. But at this price - you won't find something better."

"Are other houses even more expensive?"

"Some of them more than double! It depends. Maybe here something will change soon, at least that's what I heard. It was thought as kind of in-between solution for those who were waiting for a permanent place. But most of them stay. If you get used to it, it's not so easy to change again. - When I arrived, the manager was Miss Wally, such a beautiful warm-hearted person! I never met anybody that sweet and loving. Unfortunately she died a couple of months ago. This was a shock for all of us. Nobody had expected that. Mrs. Liebreich came just recently. Apart from her name, there is not much love around her. Sometimes I get the impression she does not know where to go. Maybe she has problems herself. I don't know. Nobody gets close to her. Maybe that's not possible. When I arrived they were talking about reconstruction, they even talked with an architect. But since then I haven't heard anything. And I must say, I am not interested in knowing. Basically - yes I can say that - I feel at home."

"And the nurse"

"Sister Erika?"

Mrs. Raiman laughed again. "I must say, that riddle I have not solved yet. But somehow I've found a way - how shall I say? - to let her be. You're right, it's not ideal, but maybe there are people with whom you can't get along. I don't know. In the beginning, I thought it was me. But now I am convinced that she has personal difficulties in her life. If you believe me or not, I have learned a lot, and I managed to accept her the way she is without wanting to change her."

Mrs. Pein listened in silence.

"Maybe I would talk differently if my son did not live nearby. If possible one of them comes every day or every other day to visit me or take me out. Either he comes himself, or his wife or one of their children. I have six grandchildren and three great grandchildren. When I am with them, believe me, there is life, and I am always glad to be back in the quietness of my own little room. At the same time I know that I won't be a burden to them. Some distance is healthy, don't you think so? Then it works fine. Then we are glad to see each other again. And in the meantime I can think about what I could do for them. It's not much, if you are bound to a wheelchair. But they had asked me a couple of times to be their baby-sitter. This was a great responsibility. But now tell me about you."

"This all came a bit too sudden for me. My daughter took me by surprise. She is in America right now. I must say, unfortunately I don't have family around. My only grandchild is studying in America, not far from Chicago. If I were twenty years younger, maybe I would have joined them. But the young people have to have their own lives. Nevertheless, I had imagined everything differently."

"Don't you have relatives?"

"Not any more. They died a long time ago. I do have one friend in the neighbourhood where I used to live, he wants to visit me as often as possible."

It was already ten o'clock and the two women were still sitting together.

The Christmas market

A couple of days later - it was around 11 o'clock - there was a knock at the door. It was Jan.

"Jan, is it you?" Esther Pein could at first hardly believe her eyes.

"My brother has to be in town now every day. Christmas market, you know. He is preparing a booth, but he did not know how to fill it. So he asked me if I could give some of my figures. I thought about you. I am sure you have an idea."

"Me? Why me?"

"I just thought. Because you are always doing some sort of craft work, for the Red Cross or church or so."

"Jan, first come in and take off the wet jacket."

"I wanted to take you along with me to show you."

"You mean - now?"

"We could eat out, for here it's not possible."

"That's a good idea, Jan, even though I don't quite understand what I could do. But it sounds interesting, that's for sure."

She took the coat out of the wardrobe, took off the slippers and put on the boots. Then she reached for her black hat.

"Is it still snowing?"

"A little. But it's not far to walk. Maybe ten minutes."

"I should tell them that I won't be there for lunch," she said, "even though I am not sure if they would notice it at all."

While leaving she looked briefly through the office window, but couldn't see anybody.

"Let's go, Jan."

The wind rattled the branches and the flakes whirled through the air. Esther Pein buttoned her coat and fastened the collar-button.

"I haven't been outside for days. How good this feels!" She took a deep breath. The road was not as busy as on the day when they visited the home for the first time. They turned into a small side street and already she could see the first couple of booths.

"That's right around the corner!" she said in surprise.

"In the evening it's even more beautiful. But right now they are just preparing. Next Sunday they want to open."

People were busy. Wires were tightened, Christmas trees decorated with electric candles. You could hear laughter and joyful voices. Esther Pein stood still in wonder and realized that she had not heard any laughter since she came to the home.

"You know, Jan, in that place you forget what it is to laugh. You can only see faces like at a funeral. And all that could be so nice!"

Jan stood in front of a small house. "Here we are."

"This is a real fairy tale house, so inviting. It reminds me of the story about Hansel and Gretel. Only the little pretzels are missing."

"We thought of that too."

"Did you design that?"

"My brother got it at an auction for a reasonable price."

"Your brother? Did he not own the furniture store on Stone street?"

"He still has that. He thought this could be a good advertisement. Only it's pretty late already, it's not much time left till Christmas, therefore he had asked me, if I would have something. That's how it came."

"And what is that?" Mrs. Pein pointed at a large, slightly stooped figure in a long coat and a broad-brimmed hat, standing on a base near the entrance. In the right hand a stick, the left holding a lantern. The eyes were looking into the far distance. "Have you made this?"

Jan nodded. "I worked the whole summer at it."

"And you did not tell me!"

"At first I did not know what it would be good for. If it gets dark, the lantern gives a dim light." Jan switched on a tiny switch inside and a warm light surrounded this figure.

"It is so inviting, that one does not want to go any further." Esther Pein admired once more the architecture from the little house and the figure in front. "Only the gingerbread is missing and red and white checked curtains and inside a warm fire."

Jan opened the door and stepped inside. Esther Pein looked around without saying a word. Along the walls were empty boards. On the floor boxes were standing around. Straw stuck out of one.

"You brought all of this here?"

"More is coming soon. My brother drove back to town to get the rest."

"And what is your plan?"

"This part is only for us to relax and warm up, if it gets too cold outside. Underneath the counter there is another heater, so we stay warm while selling." Then he pointed to the empty boards. "This all has to be filled up. And there is quite a bit missing. Therefore I had asked you."

Esther Pein examined more closely, she even knocked at the walls.

"What is it called?"

"You called it Gingerbread - that's a nice name, if you ask me."

Esther Pein laughed. "You think so? It would fit, that's for sure." She massaged her hands. "It's winter, you can feel it. It's good, that it is warm inside. What else do you have already?"

Jan opened one of the boxes.

"Some of these you know already, others are new." He took out one of the figurines and placed it on a low table. Then he took a wooden plate and a wooden lamp stand with carved-in figures.

"This is marvellous," Esther Pein said, admiring this piece of art. Then she thought again, "you know, we don't have much time left. But perhaps I could do something."

Jan looked at her. "You have an idea, haven't you?"

"I am thinking of the old people in the home. I think they need something, so their lives would get more - - more colourful. It's so grey. Sitting around, waiting for the next meal - that's not life! Can you imagine living like that ?"

Jan could not imagine.

"They are doing nothing, all day long. Some of them are not as old as I thought at first. If you take away someone's hope, Jan, that's bad. Very bad. Maybe this would help to bring back hope. But time is pretty short. I am not sure, if we can make it. If only I would have known before!"

She sat down on a chair and tried to imagine how to decorate.

"The name should be written in large letters so everybody can see."

"My brother, he could do that."

"And then, I am not sure, if I can motivate the old folks - - " She laughed, "that's strange, we are talking of 'old folks', somehow I don't count myself as being one of them. Old - that are always the other people. But I am not even the youngest there." She stopped. "What was I about to say? - - Ah, now I know. If I can talk the old people into it, then some benefit should be for them. They have to pay for the material, and I think, most of them are not rich."

"You can do what you want with the money that comes in, if that's what you mean."

"Jan, I have to think about it. For me it looks like a wonderful idea. I can hardly wait to tell them. Of course, I don't know how they would take it. Most of them don't even know the name of their neighbour next door. Only some of them know each other, and they have lived for years in the same house! I got the impression, everybody is interested only in themselves, or avoiding the other's company."

"There comes my brother Charles."

A tall gentleman in his early fifties entered. He had to bow in order not to hit the upper beam of the door.

"Esther Pein! How nice to see you here, what an honour! What do you say? The only thing that is missing, is the name."

"Gingerbread House," Jan said.

His brother looked up in surprise. "Gingerbread House, that's right. That's the perfect name!" He looked from one to the next. Jan pointed to Esther Pein, "wasn't my idea."

"That's it. Let's call it Gingerbread House. How do you like it?"

"This is marvellous! I wish I had known before!"

"I was so busy with other things, that I postponed it from one day to the next. I had mentioned it briefly to Jan and he looked for some items from his supply, but that's not enough And then, he said, he wanted to ask you."

"And what is your idea?" Mrs. Pein asked.

"To be honest, I don't have any. Maybe a sort of bazaar. As you can see, there are many different booths. One does pottery, another one weaving with a real spinning-wheel, somebody is doing some artistic paintings or photography, others are doing earrings and necklaces, somebody else comes up with knitting or cake decorating - - you name it."

"What about decorating the pots?"

"For instance."

"Or candles. You can make candles yourself from wax."

"Another idea."

"Knitting warm slippers or gloves and earmuffs."

He laughed. "I can see, you are the right person! The fantasy is without limits. What comes out at the end, nobody knows. The more original, the better."

"When I was younger, I did some batik. But that's long time ago."

"Do you still have some?"

"I am not sure. Maybe, but it would be too difficult to find them."

"You also did some embroidery or what is it called?" Jan asked.

"Bone-laces, yes, that's true. I still do that today. I am working on a table cloth right now which is nearly done. Only since I came to that house, I have not touched it."

"Do you think, you could do it?"

"To finish it? If I work on it every day, I may."

"How about inviting the two of you for lunch today. Over there is a nice rustic restaurant where we can talk in the warmth. You should not get cold," Mr. Walther said.

Esther Pein had the feeling she was dreaming. Suddenly everything was hopeful. Here was somebody who needed her. Here was a mission. She had always wished for something like that, but she did not know where to find it. And suddenly it was right in front of her feet. She only needed to start, that was all.

Together they left for the restaurant.

"It has been a long time since I was in a restaurant," Mrs Pein admitted and then added, "it's really nice. So inviting. Even a Christmas tree is there and a candle on each table."

"We will light it right away," Mr. Walther said and took some matches from his pocket. At first a timid little flame dared to come out, then slowly it stretched, still flickering, but then calming down and finally sent a warm glow.

Esther Pein ordered a salad plate and salmon in Teriyaki sauce.

"Something like that you can't get where I am," she said. "The food belongs to those things that need a reform. And I really don't know where they learned their cooking skills. But I don't want to be ungrateful."

The warmth did good. Outside it started to snow again.

"I will try right away to mobilize some folks. Maybe that's a welcome change to their dull life."

It was already 4.30 when Esther Pein returned home. She was surprised to find the door not closed. Outside it was dark. The nurse sat behind the glass panel at her desk. She looked up briefly but did not say anything and continued to type something into the computer.

80

"She did not even know that I was not here," Ms Pein thought and hurried to go back to her room. She took off her coat and the wet boots. "How do I start to motivate them?" she wondered. The best opportunity to reach everybody was during meal time. And this should be as soon as possible, for they couldn't afford to lose any time.

The bell rang for the meal. Mrs. Pein quickly washed her hands and left her room. Most of the house guests waited already in the dining hall. Some shuffled themselves forward with the help of a walker, others came with two sticks or a wheelchair, and still others came without any help.

The nurse was in charge as usual. She waited without saying a word until the last person sat down. Along the wall the girls were waiting to serve. The nurse took the little bell with the long handle in front of her and rang. Then she said a short prayer. Hardly had she said Amen, when the girls came to serve tea, followed by the familiar clacking of the cutlery.

"What filthy weather! Just the right thing for my rheumatism," said an old women opposite to Mrs. Pein. Esther Pein was wondering if this was the same person who sat beside her last evening. She was not sure. Only the rusty red colour of the short hair she had noticed. The face showed deep lines that were covered by a thick cover of rouge. The small grey eyes were deep and the pale lips were drawn downwards. "Another winter of such weather and I am under the earth."

"Did you get a flu shot as well?" the neighbour to her right asked.

"Last time it did not help. My son said after I got it I was really bad."

"I was sick three weeks after that," said an old gentleman.

Everybody had something to tell about his or her sickness and were recalling all the medicine the doctor had prescribed. That much Esther Pein had at least learned that the name of this lady opposite to her was Miss Zundel.

"I have the impression I am surrounded by medical experts," Esther Pein said with a smile.

Nobody really knew why she wanted to say that and Esther Pein regretted already that she had said it. She looked for Mrs. Raiman, but she could not see her. Maybe her son had taken her out again. At that very moment the door opened and the wheelchair with Mrs. Raiman was pushed inside. Esther Pein waved but Mrs. Raiman did not see her. Esther Pein was tempted to get up to sit beside her, but somehow she did not dare to leave her place.

She was tired of listening to this kind of talk and she herself did not know what to say. She was thinking how to cope with this weird situation.

The platter of sausage was empty again. It was not filled a second time. Only a few slices of bread were still in the bread basket and some cheese. Most of them seemed to be finished with the meal.

Mrs. Pein got up. Her heart pounded wildly. She swallowed. Then she took all her courage and said: "I would like to invite all of you this evening at 7 o'clock for a meeting in the lounge."

"Louder, I can't hear!" shouted somebody from the other end of the table.

Mrs. Pein repeated, this time louder: "I would like to invite all of you at 7 o'clock tonight for a special meeting in the lounge. It would be nice, if everybody could be there. Tonight at seven!"

Esther Pein sat down. She realized that they all stared at her. Something like that had never happened before. Mrs. Pein felt uncomfortable, mainly because of the nurse. She had the feeling as if electric waves came from that end. Mrs. Pein pretended as if nothing had happened and reached out for the bread, even though she was not hungry any more.

"Tonight at seven?" Mrs. Wise asked. "Is something special?"

"You will all like hearing that. I guess there are wonderful times ahead of us."

Mrs. Wise coughed and Esther Pein did not really know what that meant. But maybe it did not mean anything.

When Esther Pein was about to leave the dining room, the nurse called her back.

"Mrs. Pein it would be desirable if in future such kind of announcement would be made through us. If everybody would come and bring in their private ideas this would result in chaos."

"I admit, I did not think this through, and I apologise. This was a kind of emergency."

"Each kind of emergency is our responsibility."

"A Christmas-like emergency, sister Erika. And you know, around Christmas there are always secrets."

"It's about the principle."

"And which one, if I may ask?"

The nurse did not answer.

"I understand, that it is not allowed to ask a question."

The face of the nurse turned red. The eyes became like a small line, the forehead showed warning furrows, the lips were trembling. This was a sign of alarm. That meant, now you have to shut up. The nurse shook her shoulders and left.

Esther Pein looked around to greet Mrs. Raiman, but she had left already. The girls were busy cleaning the tables. Nobody paid any attention to her. Mrs. Pein did not return to her room but went directly to the lounge instead. It was dark. She switched on the light and closed the heavy curtains. Then she stepped in front of the cage.

"Can you imagine, Hansi, a real Gingerbread House? So cosy. You never saw something like that. Did you sing today? But how should you sing if nobody is there to encourage you. If only the piano would be tuned, then I would play a song for you. But wait, this too will be changed one day." She played some chords and was startled at the rattling noise. Had she really thought somebody had tuned it in the meantime? She was wondering if the piano had been tuned at all in the last fifty years. The tones were totally chaotic. She tried to play a song but could not recognise it. She lifted the lid. Was it worthwhile to work on? The frame seemed still good, and most of the little hammers had still sufficient felt left. Again she hit one key. The tone became many, running after another, embracing each other and finally left an eery echo in all directions. She closed the lid. "If they would have had that at the conquest of Jericho, they would not need to surround the city seven times. The walls would have come down immediately," she thought.

Mrs. Pein stepped to the cage. "You know, Hansi, soon people will come, lots of them. At least, that's what I hope. Probably so far nobody had seen you. Then you have to sing, will you? A real song.

For me, Hansi, please. I think, they would need it. There is no song in this house. You have to teach them how to sing."

The door opened. The first house guest entered hesitantly. "I've never been in here," said a tall gentleman. Under his right arm he had a newspaper. He looked around somehow embarrassed and with his left index finger pushed his brim-less glasses in the right position. Underneath his bushy eyebrows were deep blue eyes. White hair surrounded the smooth, shining skin of the head like a garland. Mrs.Pein introduced herself and they started a conversation.

"Your name is Guttman, if I am correct? Are you related with Fred Guttman from the local library?"

"That's me."

"Is that true? I would not have recognized you! You always served me in such a friendly way! Can you remember me?"

Mr. Guttman thought for a while, put his left hand under his chin and with his index finger stroked slowly along his lips, then he pushed his glasses up again.

"It's a while ago," Mrs. Pein came to his help.

"I am awfully sorry, but I can't remember," he admitted.

"I love books. I've been to many libraries."

"That's something that is missing in this house," he said. "But maybe nobody reads."

"You can't say that. I am a passionate reader, for instance. There is nothing more attractive for me than a good book. - What do you think, should we try to light a fire?" Mrs. Pein pointed to the fire place.

"We could try."

Mr. Guttman stepped in front of the fire place. "The wood is dry, that's fine. But I don't have paper. Wait, my newspaper here, this should be enough. There is nothing good in it anyway." He folded the paper, crumpled it and stacked some wood on top.

"What about matches?" He looked around. "Are there any matches?"

Mrs. Pein looked as well. On top of the fire place in the corner she found a small package. *Hotel Edelweiss* she could decipher. Somebody must have left it here. Some visitor from Austria? She gave him the little map with matches. The paper started to burn. The flame changed from a bluish glimmer to a reddish yellow, stretched their long fingers and greedily devoured the paper, at the same time a black cloud gradually filled the room. Mr. Guttman started to cough. The smoke brought tears to Mrs. Pein's eyes.

"The damper!" Mr. Guttman said upset, "I forgot to open the damper!"

He worked feverishly to find the switch to open the damper and pulled back his hand, that was black with soot. He cleaned it on his trousers. At that very moment the alarm went off.

"O dear, what did we do?" Esther Pein said. She hurried outside shouting, "don't worry, nothing happened, everything is all right! Don't panic!"

Several doors were opened and old people were coming out anxious and confused."

"You can go back to your room, it's a false alarm."

The alarm bell continued to scream. Mrs. Liebreich came running.

"What on earth happened?" she shouted.

Mrs. Pein tried to calm her down. "We were about to start a fire in the fire place and forgot to open the damper."

"Fire in the fire place?" Mrs. Liebreich stepped stately to the window and opened it. "Who gave you permission for that?"

"I thought where there is fire place we can start a fire," Mrs. Pein said innocently.

"But not without permission."

"When I saw the wood - -"

"That's just decoration."

"But it would spread some warmth."

"Listen, Mrs. Pein, you are taking too much freedom in this house."

"Mrs. Liebreich this house could be so different, if only - -"

Mrs. Liebreich turned and left the room. Esther Pein took a deep breath. She felt guilty. She hated this kind of feeling. But now was not the right moment to think about it. Now she had to be prepared for the next few minutes. She looked at Mr. Guttman who still knelt in front of the fire place. He poked into the fire. Mrs. Pein tried to comfort him.

"That woman needs a special instruction how to handle her. Unfortunately I don't have it," Mr. Guttman said. He took his glasses and started to wipe them clear. The he put them back on again.

"Maybe she is not so bad; after all she gave permission to keep the canary."

"Does this bird belong to you?"

"Yes. At first she did not want it."

"A difficult person, that's for sure," Mr. Guttman said.

"With a hard shell. I wish we could crack it."

Mr. Guttman laughed. "I am sure others have tried already."

"Yes, if her character would resemble her name, that would make a huge difference; but maybe she is not that unapproachable after all. Maybe we have to find out how to win her over. She does not have many friends."

"Not any!"

"At least not here."

Suddenly Mrs. Pein realized that there were not enough chairs in the room. She was wondering where to find more chairs and decided to wait and see how many would come. She shut the window and closed the curtain again.

Five minutes before seven three women came, among them Magda Wise, another neighbour whom she already met. The fire in the fire place was burning. The three women had pushed their chairs close to the fire, so they could watch the flames. Nobody dared to speak.

Now the door opened. Mrs. Raiman in her wheelchair appeared and soon after her some more entered. Mrs. Pein counted. There were still some empty chairs. But again more people came.

"I think we need a couple more chairs," Esther Pein said to Mr. Guttman and looked at her watch.

"Do you know where to find some?"

"In the hall way in front of the dining room," Mrs. Wise said.

Shortly after that he brought in more chairs and left immediately to get some more. Mrs. Pein grew excited. What did she do again? She was not prepared at all. What should she tell them? What did they expect? Suddenly she was scared. The wood in the fire place crackled. Mr. Guttman got up to put more logs on top. The flames spit blue and yellow sparks.

"Perhaps you are wondering what this is all about," Mrs. Pein started, "but first of all I would like to thank all of you for coming. I guess it's time to get to know each other better." Again the door opened and a noble white haired lady came in. Her movements were careful and restrained. A timid smile was on her lips.

"Good evening everybody," she said in a low voice and waited.

Esther Pein looked around. "If you would move closer on the sofa, there would still be room for one more person."

"Here is another chair," Mr. Guttman said and got up to offer his chair. He himself took a place on the stone bank at the fire place.

Finally everybody found a place and Mrs. Pein could continue her welcome. "I thought, since we are living in the same house together, we could well grow together like a family. For this is our family, isn't it?"

Everybody looked at her, nobody said a word.

"You know, I did not want to give a presentation here, I only wanted to tell you what had happened today and I wanted to ask your help."

Then she told about the Gingerbread House and the idea about how everybody could contribute. "And what we get from the sale, that's our money. And with this money we could do something special. Maybe a bus tour, or make a special gift for somebody. We can find that out together. I can't do that on my own. I do need all of you. It would be nice, if you could think about it and let me know. We don't have much time. But if we all work together, something good will come out of it."

Slowly life came into this group of people.

"I did a lot of needle work, when I was young. I could try again," an old woman said with a trembling voice.

"In earlier days I too did a lot, but time has changed," another woman said. There was a sadness in her voice.

"Why should this time not come back again? You could try," answered Mrs. Pein.

"But where? In my room I am not allowed to do something like that. And in this house there is no kiln and I don't have any clay either. How then could I do what I did?"

"You did pottery?"

"Until I came here."

"Do you still have some of your work?"

"More than enough."

"May I ask your name?"

"Miss Winter."

"Miss Winter, I do have a friend, who probably can help. We have to talk about it later. But I am sure, we can find a way."

Esther Pein grew more and more excited. She never thought this would happen. Her enthusiasm was contagious. The old people were all talking at the same time.

"Tomorrow we will all go together to the Gingerbread House to look. It's very close by. Just two blocks from here. And tonight everybody can think what to contribute and make suggestions. This then would become our Gingerbread Home."

At that very moment the little bird started to sing. At first timid, then more and more confident. Suddenly the old people fell silent and listened. One woman started to cry.

"It could be so different here," Mrs. Wise said, "if only sister Erika would not be here. She poisons the whole atmosphere."

"She is not the only one who is poisoning. Look at Mrs. Liebreich. I never saw her smiling. To be honest, I am afraid of her."

"Our happiness does not depend on sister Erika nor on Mrs. Liebreich. Maybe we all should try to say something nice to her."

"To these ladies? You don't know them! Her only reaction would be sarcasm. She goes like a shadow through the hall ways, looking for something she could criticize," Mrs. Wise said.

"If I hear her voice, I start trembling," an old gentleman said.

Mrs. Wise laughed: "There you can hear, even strong men are trembling!"

"She is like ice. In her presence I am freezing."

"Too bad that she can't hear what others say about her," Mrs. Pein said, "But this should not muffle our enthusiasm. Tonight is the beginning of something new. From now on we will get together regularly and talk with each other, encourage each other. I can see, you all have so much experience and so much to share. Let's seize these days of our togetherness. Tomorrow morning at 10 we will all meet at the entrance hall, or let's say - half past nine, then we go together to the Gingerbread House. But don't forget to dress warm. And tomorrow evening after supper we will meet here again. Until then everybody hopefully will come up with his or her own idea, and we will find out together what is the best to do. So, don't forget, tomorrow half past nine - after breakfast - in the entrance hall."

Mrs. Pein stretched out her hand to greet Mrs. Raiman. "Good to see you again! At least one familiar face. Seeing you, I felt more confident already. It will take a while, until I learn all these names."

"It's good, that finally somebody is here who breaks this cycle of strangeness. So, you can count on me! That's a marvellous idea!"

An idea becomes reality

At nine-twenty-five eighteen old people were already waiting in the entrance hall. Some of them armed with walking sticks, others held onto their walkers, Mrs. Raiman was waiting in her wheelchair. Mr. Guttman closed his collar to be better prepared for the cold wind.

"Ready? Then let's go!" Esther Pein said. She wore her thick blue winter coat and fur boots. Around her head she put a white shawl.

Now the elegant lady came too, who Mrs. Pein had noticed last evening for the first time. The snow white hair was partly covered by a black fur cap.

Mrs. Pein bent down to Mrs. Raiman, "Who is it?" she asked in a whisper.

"I don't know. May be a newcomer. I saw her yesterday evening for the first time."

"That's Mrs. Rosendahl," whispered Mrs. Wise who had overheard the question.

Five minutes later Mrs. Pein gave her walking stick to Mrs. Raiman, to be free to push the wheelchair. When Mr. Guttman saw that, he pushed her friendly aside and said, "Please, leave that up to me!" and took over. Mrs. Raiman was still holding the walking stick, turned to Mrs. Pein and said, "You better keep this!"

Mrs. Pein took the stick. "Let's go."

Sister Erika behind the glass window pretended not to see anything. Outside the sun was shining. The snow was glistening.

"Be careful! The sidewalk is swept but could be still slippery," Mrs. Pein said and held on to her stick.

"It would be best to hold on to each other," Miss Winter said mockingly.

"I haven't been outside for a long time," said one of the old folks. Everybody could see how she enjoyed this moment.

"The fresh air clears the lungs," Mrs. Raiman laughed.

Mrs. Pein walked beside the wheelchair and said admiringly to Mr. Guttman, "You are a gentleman of passed times. Maybe you could give the young men from today some lessons."

"I am afraid, it's too late for that," he said half amused, half resigned.

"They don't have a proper upbringing any more, that's it", said Mrs. Wise, who was trying to get closer to Mrs. Pein.

The traffic passed by. A bus drove too close to the curve, so the snow splattered.

"He should watch out better, that's what he should!" scolded Mrs. Wise.

"Now turn right," called Mrs. Pein and turned into a small side street, that was closed for cars. They could see the first booth already. Mrs. Pein realized that even more booths had been added. Soon they had reached the Gingerbread House.

"There we are," said Mrs. Pein proudly and entered the porch. She tried to open the door, but it was closed. The green window shutters with the little heart in their midst were open. She looked through the low window. The kettle on the stove was steaming.

"They will be back any moment," Mrs. Pein said. "Unfortunately here is only one bench." She pointed to the low bench underneath the window sill. "But you can look around in the meantime at the other booths."

Everywhere people were busy unpacking boxes and decorating. One could hear hammering mixed with laughter. At the neighbouring booth there was a ladder. On the upper rung a man in his blue workman's coat was standing, fastening a sleigh and reindeer. The old people watched fascinated. Next the huge Santa Claus was pinned to the chimney.

"In the evening this would look especially nice," Mr. Guttman said.

"We should come here again when it is dark," Mrs. Wise suggested.

"We will have enough opportunities to see it all. Today I just wanted to introduce you to our Gingerbread House so you have an idea.," Mrs. Pein said.

One women in her fur coat peeped through the window. "What is missing here, is a real cuckoo's clock," she said. "We made them ourselves. We had a work shop and sold them."

"Do you still have one?"

"More than one. They were called Bremer Clock."

"Why Bremer?"

"That's our name."

"Do you think, you could bring one?"

"Why not. They are just laying around. All of them are nice pieces. I will tell my son to bring us a couple."

At that moment the man came down from the ladder.

"Mr. Walther!" said Mrs. Pein in surprise. "I did not recognise you up there."

Mr. Walther laughed and greeted his guests.

"Where is Jan?" Mrs. Pein wanted to know.

"He will be back any moment, I just sent him to do some errands. He thought you would not come before ten."

"It's earlier than we thought, that's true."

Mr. Walther took his key, which was fastened to his belt, and opened the door. "It has not changed since yesterday evening," he said apologising to Mrs. Pein. "But I put up some more folding chairs. Just in case."

Mrs. Pein felt relieved when she realized that the room was heated. The stove was glowing.

"Probably a pretty expensive bill for electricity!" Mrs. Pein said.

"Not so bad. The city gives some benefits."

The old people pressed through the door. One after another came in and were looking for an empty chair, others could sit on their walker. Soon all the chairs were taken, or they sat close to each other on the benches along the walls. The floor was plain boards. The shelves reached from the floor to the ceiling and some were filled with lampshades, carved wooden plates, little colourful painted boxes, spoons and candles with golden decoration - but most of the shelves were still empty. Mrs. Rosendahl was standing in front of one shelf and looked at all the items, but she did not touch anything. Now Jan came in. At first it looked as if he wanted to go back immediately, as if he was at the wrong place. He said something, but nobody understood. Then he saw Mrs. Pein and his face brightened.

"That's my friend. Jan Walther. His brother Charles and he are the owners. This was all his idea," Mrs. Pein told her people.

Jan smiled sheepishly, stepped to the stove to warm his hands.

"We have already a cuckoo's clock," Mrs. Pein said triumphantly.

"Not only one," Miss Bremer corrected. Her cheeks were glowing.

Mrs. Pein looked around. The wheelchair was missing!

"Is Mrs. Raiman still outside?" she asked and hurried outside. There she saw that Mr. Guttman tried in vain to get the wheelchair up the steps.

"Jan, could you please help?"

Jan and his brother immediately came running and together they managed to bring in the wheelchair. They could barely make it through the door. Mrs. Raiman had to take her hands from the armrest not to get hurt. Her eyes gleaming with delight. Mr.

Guttman felt uneasy and was not so sure what to do with himself. Then he looked around as if looking for something - or somebody.

"When I was a boy we made baskets from straw, baskets of all sizes and shapes, then we sold them on the street. If I had material, I could make some," he said.

"That would be marvellous!" Mrs. Pein said. "What do you think, Mr. Walther, could we get some material for that?"

"That shouldn't be a problem. I will take care of that. I can see, it will not be difficult to furnish this place! I would never have thought to find so many helpers!"

Jan stepped to Mrs. Pein. "I have something for you," he said in a low voice and pulled a letter out of his jacket and gave it to her.

Mrs. Pein saw the sender. "You saw Helena?" she asked in an excited voice.

"Helena herself I could not see, but her mother."

Mrs. Pein opened the letter immediately and briefly looked at it, then she folded the letter again and put it into her coat.

"They want to visit us tomorrow afternoon," she told Jan. "I do hope she will bring the little one with her! Then at least I can give her the teddy." She paused and then said, "I better wait until Christmas."

"Excuse me, I still have to hang up some lights," Mr. Walter said and waved good-bye. "We will see each other more often from now on," he said while leaving.

"Jan, that's nearly like in former days. You are right in the neighbourhood."

Jan nodded. He felt helpless with so many strangers around. With his left hand he pushed his cap back, and right after that pulled it forward again. Then he started to empty the first box and put one figure after the next on the shelf.

"He made all that himself," explained Mrs. Pein.

The figures passed from one hand to another and everywhere one could hear exciting comments.

"He made all that?" Mrs. Wise asked as if she could not believe it. "They look as if they were bought."

"That's what we want," Mrs. Pein said.

Then it was time to go back. They had all seen enough to think about what they themselves could contribute.

Problems are getting bigger

When Mrs. Pein was back in her room, she had the feeling that she should go to see Mrs. Liebreich. She still felt pretty uncomfortable about what had happened the evening before. She had a bad conscience. Slowly she got the impression that she had tested the patience of Mrs. Liebreich too much. Only she had no idea what to do to get close to her. It would be best if I went there right away and tell her what we have in mind. But at the same time she knew this would not be easy. Or should she postpone a visit to another time in the future? But this would not be Esther Pein. "No, today is the best hour," she told herself. When she was about to leave her room, she saw the big teddy on her bed.

"Tomorrow I will see Helena," she told herself and a warm feeling flooded through her body. Then she left her room.

The nurse was not there. The desk looked deserted. The telephone rang four times, nobody answered. With a pounding heart she opened the door to the office. In front of the next door with the sign MANAGER she hesitated. Her hands became moist. She knocked. No answer. She knocked again. Still no answer. And yet she thought she had heard something. Carefully she opened the door. Through a gap she could Mrs. Liebreich, her head in both hands. Esther Pein did not know what to do. Should she leave and close the door without making any noise?

"Mrs. Liebreich?" she asked softly.

No response. Mrs. Pein came closer. "Are you not feeling well?" she asked concerned.

Mrs. Liebreich let her hands sink and looked at Mrs. Pein, somehow annoyed.

"Mrs. Pein."

Mrs. Pein felt guilty when she saw the red eyes, "Please, excuse me for being so rude. I did not want to disturb you. Can I do something for you?" Mrs. Pein asked disturbed.

"Since you are here, I can tell you. I don't know what to do. I am at the end of my rope. The best would be ..." She did not continue the sentence.

"Has something happened?"

"Something happened? One problem after the next. The nurse has given me her resignation, and so has the cook. From one day to the next. Such impudence. I could take them to court, both of them. But - - "

Mrs. Pein was wondering, what so say, but she did not know. She could hear the tick-tock of the big clock at the wall. Tiny sun rays danced on the dust particles.

"That's all?" Mrs. Pein heard herself say and started by her question. "I am not her counsellor," she thought. But the question came out and now she could not take it back.

"My husband wants to leave me. After 36 years of marriage. My daughter left already. I don't have anybody. Nobody. They all are glad not to see me."

Mrs. Pein sat down on a chair, opposite of Mrs. Liebreich.

"Mrs. Liebreich - - "

"Don't say a word. These are the facts. And I am sitting here not knowing what to do next."

In the hall way voices were heard. Then Mrs. Liebreich continued, as if talking to herself. "When I was young, at least I was religious. But not any more. I lost faith. And what is still left, is not enough. Maybe I should have done everything differently. But it's too late now." Mrs. Liebreich fell silent.

"But you can start anew."

"A new start? How?" She laughed loudly. "What's left is chaos."

"Chaos can become fertilizer for a new life."

"Fertilizer!" She laughed mockingly.

"As far as the cook is concerned, Mrs. Liebreich, if you ask me, that loss is not too big. We can handle that!"

"And how, if I may ask? Tomorrow for lunch something has to come to the table, and I have no idea. That's the reality!"

"The menu repeats every couple of days any way."

"With old age the taste gets lost," Mrs. Liebreich said.

"That does not mean that old people don't appreciate a good meal! Even how it's decorated is important. And what the taste concerns, I know the difference very well, if it's a good meal or just a pap."

Mrs. Liebreich stretched, "Is that an insult?" she asked with a stern voice.

Mrs. Pein regretted that she said that. Why can't she be more careful! It's always the same, the words come out without going through a sieve. She tried to calm down but then decided to be very frank.

"Mrs. Liebreich, I can see your situation. It's very difficult indeed. But I see, you don't understand. I wanted to help you, not criticise. May I be quite honest?"

"Have you ever been something else?"

Esther Pein smiled softly. "Our life always touches other lives, and the opposite is true as well. You don't have many friends in this home. To be honest, I don't know any. They would all be glad to leave this house again. But for some reason, they can't."

"So. That's what you found out. I can tell you, old people are not capable to have real feelings."

Mrs. Pein looked up in surprise. "Who told you that? Maybe an old person can't show his or her feelings easily. They have learned to hide their true feelings. Maybe it is a fear to be left alone or not to be understood. Maybe they just don't have the strength any more. Old people are like children, they are very vulnerable. They know that they need somebody, because they can't help themselves."

Mrs. Liebreich moved some pages in front of her on the desk. Then she closed the binder, put the pen aside and drummed with her fingers on the desk. "Why do I listen to you at all!"

"Mrs. Liebreich, our life is too short, let's make friends."

"Make friends," Mrs. Liebreich repeated. "For that it's too late. At my age you can't make friends any more."

"That what you think. I myself want to make many friends. And I am some years older than you."

"A friendship must grow. That needs time. And time is something I don't have."

"Its not that important how many years are left, but how we are using the time that is entrusted to us. Maybe it's not always easy to love people. I admit. Some show a hard shell, but often underneath I have seen a soft kernel. People want to be loved and they want to love - like you, Mrs. Liebreich."

"Who told you that I am interested in being l-o-ved!" While saying that she stretched the word love so Esther Pein could hear the sarcasm in her voice.

"If you don't feel this longing deep inside of you then you are either not a human being - or you are sick."

"That's enough, Mrs. Pein! I have lost far too much time talking to you. Please, excuse me!"

Mrs. Pein remained seated. She stared to the floor and said in a low voice. "Maybe I hurt you and now you want to make yourself strong. But if we can show our vulnerability, it shows that we are human beings."

"Mrs. Pein, I have work to do!"

Mrs. Pein stood up and left the office.

My Dodo doesn't want me

When Mrs. Pein got to her room, a housemaid was busy putting a new cover on the neighbouring bed.

"Is Miss Baumgarten coming back? Esther Pein asked.

"I am not sure, but I don't think so."

Shortly after that the door opened and the nurse entered together with an old woman, about eighty years old, that was anxiously looking around.

"That is Mrs. Long," the nurse said and put the bag on the carpet. She was about to leave the room again when the old lady took hold of her sleeves.

"Where is my daughter?" she asked with a tearful voice.

"She is coming with the luggage."

Mrs. Pein felt taken by surprise. Nobody told her that a new neighbour would come. She was relieved finally to be on her own in the room and now had to cope again with a stranger. She looked briefly at the new comer. The old woman stood in the room without moving, her hands were trembling. She wore a loose hanging jacket on top of wide checked trousers. The hair didn't seem to be her own. They were too perfectly curled and the colour did not appear to be natural. The cheeks were powdered with a strong rouge, her eyes were signed by dark shadows. Mrs. Pein stepped towards her.

"My name is Esther Pein."

"My Dodo doesn't want me anymore," the old woman started to lament. "She doesn't want me anymore."

"Is that your daughter?"

The old woman nodded. "And she has such big house. She has room for her two dogs and her friend, but not for her old mother. The old mother can be put into a home, so they can enjoy their lives."

Mrs. Pein was wondering what to say, but she could not find the right words.

"I will go home to my Dodo. I didn't do anything to her."

The small face grew even smaller. A deep sadness darkened her face and wrapped her whole appearance.

"Shall I help to unpack your things?"

"No, my daughter is doing that." She wiped away some tears with a handkerchief and blew her nose.

"Don't you want to take off your jacket?"

"I don't know. I don't want to. How can she do this to me?"

Esther Pein shook her shoulders and busied herself at the wardrobe. She was angry and could not tell why. Maybe because she could not be on her own anymore. Then the daughter came with a gentleman. Her black shiny leather coat reached nearly to the floor. It was not buttoned. Underneath was a red sweater with a braided golden necklace. A strong flavour of violets filled the air, that hardly covered the smell of cigarettes.

"There you are, Mimsh," the young lady said and did not even realize the presence of Mrs. Pein. Only her companion nodded briefly.

"Where shall we put that?" he asked pointing to the suitcase.

The daughter looked around. "Is that your wardrobe, Mimsh?"

"I don't know."

"Where can my mother store her things?" the daughter asked Mrs. Pein. Mrs. Pein was surprised about the deep voice.

"This is for both of us, the left part is empty and over there is a storage room for the suitcase."

"You see, everything is fine," the daughter said and opened the door of the wardrobe. The cold leather coat touched Mrs. Pein and made her shiver. The high black boots reached to the knee, when she bowed down, the white, narrow seated jersey trousers could be seen. Mrs. Long did not move. The daughter took the suitcase and put it on the bed of Mrs. Pein without asking, opened it and took out the first dress. It was a long dress with black and white dots. She put it on a hanger, then turned to her mother.

"You have time enough to unpack, and I am sure your new roommate will help. I have to go."

Mrs. Long started to cry.

"Be a good girl. And don't forget, we are paying 2,500 Dollars each month."

"We?" Mrs. Long asked under sobs.

The daughter looked at her friend, then kissed her mother on the forehead and left. The perfume was still hanging in the air after she had left. The old mother went to the window and followed the two of them with her eyes.

"They didn't even look back once," she said. "They are glad to get rid of me."

Mrs. Pein thought of Britta, her own daughter. How was she doing, she was wondering. She had not heard from her for a while, but at the same time, she was so busy that she did not even miss her.

"It's important to live one's own life," Mrs. Pein said.

Mrs. Long let the curtain go. "What do you mean?"

"Our children need their own space to live their lives."

"I never thought about myself, I did everything for my daughter, I have sacrificed everything for her."

"Is that not what we as parents should do? Do you expect something in return?"

"To be there for me in my old age, is that too much to ask?"

Mrs. Pein felt helpless. What should she say? How often was selfish expectation behind all the good work. Where was this love that forgot oneself, giving without wanting something in return. What is love? she wondered, the pure love that gives itself and seeks the best for somebody else. "Maybe we humans are not capable to give this kind of love, unless we are touched by divine love, and this love changes our heart. But as long as a person is rooted in this world, he will take water from a dry well and always will remain thirsty for love."

"And that before Christmas," Mrs. Pein heard again this wailing voice.

"Perhaps this time will be a big chance for you."

"What do you mean?" Mrs. Long asked irritated and blew her nose.

"To learn something new. Difficulties are always a special challenge. Through difficulties we learn the most."

"I don't need any. I've had enough. Being old is a curse, I tell you, a curse."

"If a curse or a blessing that depends on us."

"But I didn't do anything to her. I can't understand. How can she do that to me? I didn't deserve this!"

Mrs. Pein realized that her words did not reach her. Words would not lift her up out of her misery. Were all these people here not prisoners, prisoners longing for freedom. She thought of sister Erika and Mrs. Liebreich. Everybody was bound in her own way. Chained to self. They could not free themselves to give freely so others could receive. And she herself still had so much to learn. The happiest times were, when she was able to forget herself. But this was not a program, she could learn. It was a gift.

Mrs. Long started to unpack her suitcase. She was standing in front of the wardrobe.

"That's far too small. My stuff would not fit in here!"

"This is one possibility to look at things."

"What do you mean?"

"We still have far too many things at our age that we are carrying along. Things we don't really need."

"That is not stuff! I do need this. All of it!" Mrs. Long said reproachfully.

Mrs. Pein was startled. Again she said something before thinking. She had to learn to separate thinking and speaking. Often she said something she later on regretted and wished she had never said. And that in her old age. She thought about the conversation with Mrs. Liebreich. How she wished she would not have said that. "Maybe I could have reached out to her, if I would have handled the whole situation differently." And the more she thought about it, the more miserable she felt. "Oh God, when will I reach the point that I say only what I am supposed to say?"

"Could you put all your things in here, Mrs - - Mrs - - I forgot your name."

"Pein. Esther Pein. No of course not. To be honest, I had four times as much as you have. Most of the things my daughter took home again. We need less than we think."

"Nevertheless, that's not enough space." She put another dress into the wardrobe. "How is it in here? Do you like it?"

"I guess it always depends what we do in a certain situation. For one person a home can become a prison, for another it becomes a home."

"And the people here?"

"Like you and I."

"At what time is supper?"

"Five o'clock. Two hours. from now."

"Can I come with you?"

Mrs. Pein was holding her breath for a second. She did not want to feel pressed. She wanted to be free. But then she said,

"Sure, we can go together."

Helena

Esther Pein waited in the entrance hall. She had to admit that she had fled out of her room. She could not take it any longer. She felt helpless. What should she say? It was good that Helena was coming. This brightened her day. She looked at her watch. It could not take much longer. "How is it possible that I am looking forward that much to a child that is not even my own? She could be my great grand child. Maybe she reminds me of Britta in her childhood. Only Britta had blond hair and freckles, while Helena is a black curly head. I believe there they are." But when she looked closer, she knew that she was wrong.

She sat down on the bench in the entrance hall again and watched the street. A car stooped immediately in front of the house and two muffled figures stepped out, a woman and a child. The car moved on again. The child stood and looked around as if looking for something. Esther Pein got up and opened the heavy door and waited. As soon as the child saw her, she let go the hand of her mother and came running up the stairs. Mrs. Pein embraced her and stroked the black curls. Then she reached out her hand to greet Mrs. Venicetti. Above the long brown trousers she wore a fur jacket. The collar was closed. The white knitted cap was pulled deep into her face.

"Cold outside," Mrs. Venicetti said and shook hands. "My husband is coming as well, he is just looking for a parking spot."

"Then we will wait right here."

"Good to see you again, Mrs. Pein. Helena was like crazy when she heard we were going to visit you, she could hardly wait."

"I made something for you," Helena said proudly and showed Mrs. Pein a little doll made from felt. "So that you are not lonely any more. Mom told me, you are lonely here."

Mrs. Pein admired the doll. "She can even roll her eyes!"

Helena was delighted. "Such eyes you can buy, you know?"

"Tonight she will sleep with me in my bed."

"Then you won't be afraid anymore. I don't want to go to bed when it's dark. I am scared. Are you scared too?"

"Sometimes. Old people and children should sleep a lot."

"Our cat too. She always sleeps. Do you live here?"

Before she could answer, Mr. Venicetti came. She saw him today for the first time. At first she was a bit embarrassed and did not know what to say.

"I would rather invite you to my own home," she said, "but I can't help it. It is nice that you came. It would be best if we go to the lounge."

Mrs. Pein went first. Helena skipped beside her and reached out her little hand so Mrs. Pein could hold it and chatted happily.

"I have not seen you for such a long time. You never came to the ducks. I was there every day. But you were not there. I was looking for you. Sometimes I forgot the crumbs, then I could not feed them. When are you coming back?"

"I hope soon. Are the ducks still there? It's so cold!"

"They don't freeze, mother said. They have a thick coat with oil, so the water does not go through. They can even swim in the icy water."

"Is that so?"

"You can make a hole in the ice, then they swim."

The temperature in the lounge was pretty low. Mrs. Pein tested the electrical heater and tried to reset it. But somehow it did not work. Helena had discovered the bird cage and stepped in front of it. The canary fluttered anxiously up and down.

"You have to be very careful, Helena, this little bird is scared of you," Mrs. Pein said and stepped beside the child. "This bird is so tiny like - like - give me your hand - even smaller than your hand. And when it sees you, in his eyes you are like a giant, standing in front of his cage. Wouldn't you be afraid as well, if suddenly a giant is standing at your bed side?"

Helena nodded.

"If this little bird would be free, it could fly away, but here it can't run away to hide itself."

"Is his name Hansi?"

While Mrs. Pein was talking the little bird calmed down.

"Does it belong to you?" Helena asked without letting the canary out of her eyes.

"Yes, I brought him from home."

"I would like to have a bird also. But Mom said, we can't. We have a cat. Why is he in a cage?"

"If he would not be in a cage, he would fly away and outside he would freeze to death."

"May I feed him?"

"There is enough food in this feeding dish."

"Do you have to feed him every day?"

"Sure. You want to eat every day as well, wouldn't you?"

"Helena, that's enough," her mother called. "Please, excuse us, Mrs. Pein."

"Not at all! I really enjoy listening to her! I am so glad you came. But please, take a seat. Maybe here on the sofa?" Mrs. Pein got an additional chair and sat down.

"We had planned to take you out for a meal, but to be honest, we are still in a shock," Mrs. Venicetti said.

"Shock? What kind of shock?"

She hesitated and looked at her husband, who stared to the floor. "Did I tell you that my husband lost his job?"

Mrs. Pein thought for a while but could not remember.

"Two months ago," Mrs. Venicetti continued. "Just from one day to the next. We never had thought something like that would happen. They had promised him another job and we waited from one week to the next, but just now we learned that somebody else got his job."

"I am sorry to hear that."

Mr. Venicetti looked down embarrassed and played with his hands. Mrs. Venicetti tried to comfort him.

"There are many experiencing the same nowadays. You are still young," Mrs. Pein said.

"Young? That's what you say!"

"What was your job?"

"I was a cook in an Italian restaurant."

"A cook?" Mrs. Pein suddenly got exited. "And now you are looking for a job?"

"You know how it is nowadays. I went from one restaurant to the next asking for a job. But nobody - nobody would need me."

"Do you have a certain expectation as far as your job is concerned?"

"I would be satisfied with whatever, if only I would find something. You are not a human being without a job, especially as a man. A man would like to provide for his family. And when you are young and you see that you can't take care of your own family - - "

"Please, excuse me for a moment!"

Ten minutes later Mrs. Pein came back with Mrs. Liebreich. Mrs. Pein introduced her friends. Mrs. Liebreich examined Mr. Venicetti from head to toe and asked: "Mr. Venicetti, would you be willing to work in an old people's home?"

"What do you mean?"

"As a cook? Our cook had unexpectedly resigned and we don't have anybody."

"And you thought, I - -"

"Just an idea."

Mr. Venicetti jumped up. "I can't believe it! Mrs. Liebreich, do I dream? Did you really say that? I could work right here?"

"The kitchen was a bit of a problem anyway, and I don't want to talk about it. What would you be able to cook, Mr. Venicetti?"

"Just call me Toni."

"What would you like to cook, Toni?"

"Let's see. Pesce for example or Scampi Royal, Calamari, Gnorrchi, Risotto, Prosciutto, Tiramisu, Panasotta, Rigatoni all Arrabiata - - " He pressed thumb and index finder of his right-hand together and pressed them to his lips and gave a clicking noise, moved his arm toward Mrs. Liebreich and said, "Prima-primissimo, I tell you, first class, hhhmmm!"

Mrs. Pein felt the water gathering in her mouth. She laughed. Mrs. Liebreich did not change her feature.

"When could you start?" she asked.

Toni rolled up his sleeves. "If you ask me, at once! But it would be good to see the kitchen."

"The kitchen? Of course, without a kitchen you can't cook. Come with me."

"Helena, please wait, we will be back in a moment," Mrs. Venicetti told the child and got up as well.

"Could you watch Hansi in the meantime?" Mrs. Pein asked.

"But don't let him out of the cage," her mother told her. "We are just going to see the kitchen, then we will be back again."

"I'll wait," Helena said.

Mrs. Liebreich went ahead, Toni, Mrs. Venicetti and Mrs. Pein followed. In front of an iron door with a large sign "Keep out!" Mrs. Liebreich waited. It was the first time that Mrs. Pein was allowed to see this "holy" place. She felt somewhat uncomfortable. Maybe because of the threatening sign, she had never dared to come even close. But sometimes she was tempted. The huge heating plate was clean. All the cupboards closed.

"May I?" Toni asked and opened one of the doors. There were shiny pots. He opened one drawer. Everything was neat and in order. Above the counter large spoons were hanging and underneath knives in all sizes. "Looks as if I could start right away." He briefly looked into the cool room where huge chunks of meat were hanging. "And where are the spices?" he asked and opened one cupboard after the next. He could not find any. Also nothing close to the fan above the stove. Just salt in a glass bowl and sugar.

"Maybe here?" Mrs. Pein opened another door, leading into a store room. There was a shelf stacked with tins, all ready made food, and some glasses with fruit and canned cucumbers. On the floor a sack with flour and another one with potatoes. But no spices.

"This will change, I promise!" said Toni.

"To this job belongs an apartment as well," Mrs. Liebreich said.

"This can't be true! No, this can't be true. I must be dreaming!"

"It's not a very big one, but if you agree, you could move in right away. It belongs to the house, the upper floor. Three bed rooms, kitchen and bath."

"Mrs. Liebreich. I really don't know what to say. In my eyes, it is a miracle. So the Lord had answered our prayers."

Mrs. Liebreich turned to Mrs. Venicetti. "You are not by chance a nurse?"

"I am a mid wife."

"We are looking for a nurse as well." Mrs. Liebreich closed the heavy doors to the kitchen.

"Mrs. Liebreich, if I can be of any help, I would love to. I always wished I could work with old people. I just love old people."

"We can talk about that later. As soon as you are here, we will see what we can do."

Visit at the hospital

After Toni started working in the kitchen everybody realized immediately that somebody else was in charge. The family was supposed to move in next week, then Helena would be here too. Everything looked so much brighter now.

"Being surrounded with young life makes a big difference," Mrs. Pein said to her room mate.

"If there is not too many of those," Mrs. Long answered.

Mrs. Pein kept silent. She was surprised that every positive comment was poisoned with a negative response. She took the coat from the wardrobe, then the white shawl and put it on.

"You are going away?"

"I am visiting a friend in the hospital."

When Mrs. Pein entered the hospital, she had the feeling a cold hand was clasping her throat. She hardly dared to walk, fearing her steps could echo in the long hall way. At the desk she was told that Miss Baumgarten was on the 6th floor. The elevator door opened with a squeaky noise.

Along the hallway beds on wheels were lined and carts with piled towels and linen and all kinds of cleaning material, also a bag with used cloths could be seen. Then the hall way widened into a niche with a high counter. A nurse was sitting in front of a computer and typed in something. A male nurse came with a tray full of medicine. The little glasses were filled with colourful pills, some with a white liquid.

"I would like to see Miss Baumgarten," Mrs. Pein said in a low voice.

"Room No 603. But you have to wait, until the doctor's visit is over."

Mrs. Pein waited. Shortly after that the door opened. Several men and women in white left the room and went to the next room, talking loudly. With her heart pounding Mrs. Pein entered the room. At first she could not see Miss Baumgarten. She counted six beds, all the same iron frames with high metal gallows at the head. From some of them plastic bottles were dangling, being connected with the arm of a person, from others a leather sling. Each bed resembled a small island, only separated with a plastic curtain from the neighbouring bed. The curtain around the last bed was closed. Mrs. Pein stepped closer and whispered: "Miss Baumgarten?"

A women in the first bed pointed with her hand to the bed opposite her. The bed sheet covered the whole person. Mrs. Pein could just see a bump and a naked white arm that was connected to some tubes. On the monitor some lights were flickering. Miss Baumgarten slowly moved her head.

"It's me, do you recognise me? Esther Pein."

Miss Baumgarten thought for a while, then apparently she remembered. She tried to sit up, but sank back again onto her pillow.

"Mrs. Pein, how nice of you to come."

Esther Pein took a small parcel out of her pocket. "Everybody in the home sends you greetings. As soon as you are back we have to show you all the news. There are some changes going on!"

"Changes? Nothing had changed in all those years."

Then Mrs. Pein told about the Gingerbread House that kept them all so busy.

"I can't imagine. Every day was just the same old story. Without any excitement. Like a grave side."

"We even have a new cook!"

"You don't say!"

They both fell silent for a while. Then Miss Baumgarten said, "I never thought it would hit me. You know what I thought? If I am gone, nobody would follow my coffin. Maybe somebody from the home, but only because this is the custom. Otherwise nobody. My life did not make a difference for anyone."

Mrs. Pein did not say a word. She tried to say something, but all the words just did not fit. Then she saw on the little night table the book she had given her before she left. She took it.

"Did you look through?"

"Not yet."

Stories and still more stories, Mrs. Pein read. "There is a nice one, would you like to hear?"

"Why not?"

Mrs. Pein turned the pages, until she found what she had looked for.

"Could you please read a bit louder, so we can listen as well?" one woman in the opposite bed said.

Mrs. Pein looked a bit doubting. "If you like?"

"Sit down, there is a chair," the woman said again.

Mrs. Pein took the chair and sat beside the bed of Miss Baumgarten.

"The story is entitled: *One day only*..."

One Day Only

Three heavenly messengers were concerned about what they saw happening on earth and had only one wish to visit the earth and change the world. The Creator of the Universe agreed and allowed them to visit the earth just for one day. The first messenger decided to go to parliament to influence world politics. The second wanted to change the media, for, as he told himself, a new influence from there would make a big difference for millions. The third wanted to go into industry to stop the manufacture of weapons; then peace on earth would finally come, or so he hoped. Each of the heavenly messengers received a one hundred dollar bill to buy themselves something to eat, for as soon as they came to earth they would become humans, feeling hungry like all the others.

Soon the first messenger reached the capital. It did not take him long to find the government building. But when he was about to enter it, he slipped and broke his leg. He was in pain and could not move. Finally the gardener found him and took him to a nearby hospital. There he had to stay until dark.

The second messenger came to a remote area where he met a boy who sat under a bridge crying.

"Why are you crying?" the angel asked.

"Somebody stole the grocery money mother gave me. It was all we had. Now I am afraid of going home to tell my mother."

"Take this," the angel said and gave him the hundred dollars. "I can walk to the city," he told himself. But when he reached the city it was dark already and he did not have time to do what he wanted to do.

The third angel came to a big city with fuming chimneys. He knew exactly where to go, for he had studied every detail of his journey before. In front of an iron gate he heard a soft moan. When he looked more closely he saw an old woman.

"Why are you crying?" he asked.

"They took my daughter. And I don't know where they have taken her." Then she told him how soldiers had stormed her house and taken the girl with them.

"Don't worry, I'll find your daughter and bring her back," the angel said. He searched until it was dark. Then he found the girl in a forest, tied to a tree, bleeding and bruised. He loosened the rope, lifted her carefully on his shoulders and carried her back home to her mother. Since it was late already he gave her the hundred dollars and said, "Take this for yourself and your daughter, so you won't have to go hungry."

When the time came for the three messengers to return they were very discouraged and sad since they hadn't succeeded in what they had set out to do.

"Lord of the Universe," the first one stammered, "please, forgive me, I didn't finish my task."

"What did you do?"

"I can't even tell. I have done nothing, nothing at all. Before I could start it was dark already."

"And what did you do with the hundred dollars?"

"I gave them to the gardener who found me."

The second angel came forward. He hardly dared to look up.

"Forgive me, Lord of Heaven and Earth. I didn't accomplish anything. Before I reached the city my time was over."

Now the third angel fell down on his face and said sorrowfully,

"Lord of the Universe, I wanted to bring peace to earth, but I couldn't even get to those in power. I haven't accomplished anything. Please, forgive me."

Then the Lord let them look down on the earth.

"Do you see this man?" God asked the first messenger.

"He was in the hospital, right next to me in the other bed. I know him."

"He had planned a crime. He wanted to kill thousands of people. But when he told you about his childhood you cried. Your tears touched him so deeply that he became another man. The day you spent on earth was not in vain."

Then the Lord called the second angel and showed him a young man, who walked through the villages of Africa, healing the sick.

"Do you know this man?"

When the angel looked he recognised the boy to whom he had given the hundred dollars.

"This boy was so impressed by what you did that he decided to become a missionary, to help those who couldn't help themselves. The day you spent on earth was not in vain."

The third angel was still lying on the ground and didn't look up.

"I have failed," he said, "nothing has changed through me."

Then the Lord showed him a big house with many children. "Do you know this woman?"

Somehow her face seemed familiar, and suddenly he realized that it was the same woman whose daughter had been taken away by the soldiers.

"Because you saved her daughter, she decided to devote her life to orphans. She became a mother to many, who would otherwise have been lost. The day you spent on earth was not in vain."

Then the three messengers bowed down, radiant with joy and wonder.

It was very quiet in the room. Then Miss Baumgarten said, "To think that I don't have much time left, that scares me. But when I think about what you read, I think, maybe life is still worth living."

"If we live only for ourselves, time is lost, but if we use the time for others, it's worth living," Mrs. Pein said, and quietly added, "Even if it was only one hour that we spent on earth and the love of God could reach another person through us, it was not in vain."

Mrs. Pein as match-maker

When Mrs. Pein returned to the lounge two days later, Mr. Guttman was already busy with the fire.

"This time I did not forget the damper!" he said with a smile and pushed his glasses in place.

Mrs. Pein looked at him and could not help thinking that something was troubling him. He turned his back to her as if to avoid looking at her. She was wondering what it could be. But she had no idea and did not want to ask him either.

That evening more than twenty people came. She would never have thought that so many ideas would come together. And what was even better, all these people were enthusiastic about it. On the table the first items could be seen, even with a price tag.

Mrs. Rosenstock sat in a corner of the sofa, silently working on a white stole with a beautiful pattern. Mrs. Pein watched her and was wondering what kind of profession she might have had. The white wavy hair was held together in a knot. The facial lines emanated a soft elegance. Perhaps she was a doctor, she thought. But she did not want to ask, her whole appearance was withdrawn. When they met last time, she had briefly mentioned her name, but did not tell anything about herself. That much she remembered, that her name was Judith Rosenstock. Somehow the name fitted her and she wished to get to know her more. She was very tastefully dressed but unobtrusive. She always wore a long dark skirt with a white blouse. By chance she looked at Mr. Guttman and realized that he secretly watched her, then quickly looked aside. But something in his look made her wonder if they knew each other? Then they would speak to one another, but she never saw the two talking.

Miss Bremer bent over the table to look closer at a pottery. "Did you make that?" she asked "I would never have thought it!"

Miss Winter was flattered and smiled.

"There are many hidden talents among us," Mrs. Pein said.

"I never thought I would enjoy anything anymore. I thought "that's it. It's over." But life is not as bleak as I thought. Somewhere there are still some bright spots," Miss Winter said and started to paint another piece of pottery.

"It's black for me. I wouldn't know what the bright spots are in my life. I have Parkinson's Disease. What's nice about that?"

Everybody stared at Mr. Muller.

"Black as the night."

Mrs. Pein thought of what she could say. "Maybe we can't see the bright side," she said.

"If you ask me, we are talking far too much about sickness," Mrs. Raiman said.

Mr. Muller was hurt. Mrs. Pein tried to save the situation and said, "We all have our own load on our shoulders. Let's try to carry the load of each other. It's good to have the opportunity to talk, but each complaint should finally turn into some positive thought to lift us all up."

"That's easy to say. If you were in my shoes, you would not say that," Mr. Muller insisted.

At that moment Miss Baker entered the lounge. With her hands slightly stretched she tried to feel her way. The blind eyes were wandering restlessly to and fro. Mr. Guttman got up to lead her to his chair. He sat down again close to the open fire on the stone bench.

"I too have something to give," she said and pulled out of her pocket some crocheted pot gloves.

Mrs. Pein took them. "You made this yourself? How could that be?"

The gloves went from one person to the next. Miss Baker smiled sheepishly, and her face appeared years younger.

"If I still had my own kitchen, I would order some right away," Miss Bremer said.

The door was opened briefly and immediately shut again.

"Sister Erika," somebody whispered. At that moment there fell a spell over the room.

"Somebody should give her a mirror so she can see herself," Miss Winter said in a low voice.

"I don't know, if that would help," Mrs. Raiman said.

"Sister Erika won't be with us any longer," Mrs. Pein said and was startled when she said that. Maybe it was too early to tell. Voices hummed all at once.

"I can't believe that."

"She will survive all of us."

"I can't imagine this house without that scarecrow."

"Perhaps we don't know her," Mrs. Pein said.

"We don't know her?" Mrs. Wise asked with a sharp voice.

"Maybe she suffers the most herself but she can't help it," Mrs. Pein said.

"If she would leave, that would be the best thing that could happen," Miss Baker said while the long knitting needles danced.

Nearly two hours had passed. Slowly the room became empty. Now Mrs. Rosenstock also folded her needlework and got up. She had not said a word the whole evening. Mrs. Pein looked at the skilful crafted stole.

"That is a masterpiece. I can see you are not doing something like that for the first time."

Mrs. Rosenstock smiled and Mrs. Pein thought, how beautiful she looks. The few lines gave her face a certain dignity. There was no artificial colour added to her cheeks or eyebrows. A warm smile played around her lips.

"Thanks," she said simply.

"You are rich. Who ever is able to do this, is rich."

"eisehu aschir? hasameach bechelko - who is rich? who is content with his part, our rabbi always says."

Mrs. Pein would have loved to talk some more with her, but she did not want to appear obtrusive.

Mr. Guttman stood up and stirred the fire to extinguish the last sparks.

"Good night," Mrs. Rosenstock said.

"See you tomorrow," Mrs. Pein answered.

When Mrs. Rosenstock left, Mr. Guttman followed her with his eyes. Again Mrs. Pein had the feeling he wanted to say something. She was standing at the door, ready to turn off the light. Mr. Guttman looked at her but did not move. Again he pushed up his glasses.

"You are not tired yet?" Mrs. Pein asked.

"Not yet."

"Can't you sleep?"

"Not much."

"Do you take something?"

"I try to avoid that. Only from time to time valerian."

"One night can be very long."

"Indeed," he said and started to set the chairs in order.

"What do you think about our progress?"

"They all seem to enjoy it."

"I think so too. What about you?"

"I can't contribute anything. Somehow I feel out of place."

"We do need a master fireman."

Mr. Guttman smiled. "That's not much. Others can do that as well. You know, sometimes I have the feeling I am from a different planet. I don't belong. I am a stranger. Everywhere. I can't share their enthusiasm. Sometimes I read the newspaper, then again I put it down. That's not my world. But where am I at home, I wonder."

They both fell silent for a while. Each had his or her own thoughts.

"Mrs. Pein - -"

She waited.

"Do you know Mrs. Rosenstock?"

"A very fine lady."

"I mean, do you know her really?"

"Not yet. Why?"

"I just wondered." Again he pushed up his glasses.

Mrs. Pein was surprised, took a chair closer and sat down. "Is there something you want to tell me?"

"Not really. I am not even sure if she knows my name. She was a musician. Pianist."

"What do you say!"

"I heard her once playing in the symphony the 4th piano concert from Beethoven. I never heard this piece before. It was wonderful."

"I did not know that."

"Mrs. Pein, this may sound stupid - but could you perhaps - could you arrange it somehow - -" He did not finish the sentence. Slowly Mrs. Pein understood.

"You would like to get to know her and don't know how?"

He smiled.

"If that's all, Mr. Guttman, I would like to get to know her myself as well. She is a pianist, you said?"

"Yes."

Mrs. Pein stepped to the piano and opened the cover. "It's not a Bechstein, that's for sure, but perhaps something could be done. What do you think about an evening of music? We even could invite the public for such a concert, through the paper. Why not? But first a tuner has to fix it. But this then is your job. Only, I don't dare to ask Mrs. Liebreich. For the time being she is fed up with me, I guess."

"I will pay for the cost."

"Good. Then take care that the piano is being tuned, and I will take care of the rest."

"Mrs. Pein - -"

"Mr. Guttman?"

"It's stupid maybe. What should you think about me. I don't want you to tell anybody."

"Tell what? About the concert?"

"No, of course not, what I told you - -"

"But this is a fantastic idea!"

"I see, you don't understand. It's not because of the piano, it's because of the lady."

"You like her?"

He blushed. Mrs. Pein could not hide a smile, but tried to be serious.

"You are in love with her?"

"What would you think at my age." He pushed his glasses higher.

"What do you mean 'at my age'. Have you been married before?"

"No. I always was single."

"You never fell in love?"

"Maybe once."

"And why did you not marry her?"

He looked down. "I did not dare to ask her."

"You never told her that you loved her?"

"Never. And one day she married somebody else."

"And that was it for you?" Mrs. Pein shook her head. "It's not too late. Is she single?"

"She is a widow with a daughter, who is married."

"I can see you did your home work already."

"What should you think about me!"

"I am glad you told me. I feel honoured."

"You are not laughing?"

"Why should I?"

"You wouldn't say anything to anybody?" Mr. Guttman took his glasses and started to clean them vehemently with his handkerchief.

"Only with your permission, that much I can promise. I will try to push a bit from behind. But - the piano tuner is your responsibility."

"I will do it. Tomorrow first thing in the morning," Mr, Guttman said and put on his glasses again.

Christmas preparations

In the lounge large baskets were standing everywhere to store all kinds of craftwork. Mr. Walter brought some twigs and since the gym was never used, it became the store room and workshop. Jan was able to get some clay, they had only to find a kiln. The store owner told him he would take care of the kiln firing. However, he could find a potter wheel. Mrs. Raiman had finished some bread baskets already and an egg basket. Now she was busy with a shopping basket. She was sitting in front of the fire place with red cheeks. Mrs. Pein watched the skilled movements.

"I can see you are well trained in that."

"What you learned, it stays," Mrs. Raiman said and smiled. "I have not used those hands for years and I am surprised myself that the fingers still know what to do. You know, before I got sick, we always decorated the house with branches. Together with my children we made hundreds of stars with straw. This was always the highlight of the year. But now everything has passed," she said sadly.

Mrs. Pein thought for a while. "Why should it be over? That's a marvellous idea. In a couple of weeks it's Christmas and you can't see it in this house at all. As soon as Mr. Walther comes, I will ask if he could bring us some branches."

"Maybe he also knows where to get some straw. We always put the stalks in water to soften them and after we ironed them it was easy to use them."

"I must admit that I am not very skilled in that kind of job. I would rather take over the organizing part," Mrs. Pein said.

"I could never do that. I am happy to work with my hands."

Now Mrs. Wise came with a blue-white shopping bag and placed it dramatically on the table. Her cheeks were glowing.

"Would you like to see?" She pulled a beautiful little romper out of the bag and a matching cap and gloves and tiny shoes. Everywhere exiting voices were heard. Mrs. Wise said proudly, "Next I will make a jacket. Everything in pink."

"Only the baby is missing!"

"I totally forgot how much pleasure this gives."

"We could make a wreath and put it right here with some candles," Mrs. Raiman suggested.

"And one for the door," Mr. Guttman said. Everybody looked up in surprise. It was the very first time that he said something in this circle.

"It's time to bring everything to the Gingerbread House. Have you seen how it looks now?" Mrs. Pein asked.

"I've been there this morning. It looks so inviting," Mrs. Wise said.

"Jan did everything to make it as nice as possible so we can have a cup of coffee and warm up."

"But you should see it at night, everywhere along the roof line are colourful bulbs, that spread a warm light. Even along the counter there is a garland with tiny stars," Mrs. Pein said.

"You said we will start tomorrow?" Miss Baker asked.
"Tomorrow, yes. Some of the booths are opening a few days later, but the official beginning is tomorrow afternoon."

"Are we going to sell the stuff ourselves?" Miss Bremer asked.

"Surely. Everybody who likes to. We came up with a timetable." Mrs. Pein showed a large paper with lines and numbers. "Everybody who wants to be involved can put her or his name in here with the time, so it won't get too much for one person. We thought, if everybody could be available for two hours, that will do."

The timetable was passed from one person to the next. Not everybody felt comfortable, but most of them listed their name at least for one hour. After that everybody busied themselves with their particular job. In between one could hear laughter.

"Are men allowed as well?" Mr. Guttman asked.

"Only with a written permission," Mrs. Pein said mockingly.

"Tell me somebody about the weaker sex," Mr. Guttman mumbled.

Everybody laughed.

"Ladies, I am very proud of you, just continue with the same effort," Mr. Gerber said.

"To judge others and do nothing, that's what you like, do you?" Mrs. Pein said.

"Somebody has to fire on the troop, don't you agree?" he said with a twang.

"I guess you had been a foreman somewhere?" Mrs. Raiman said mockingly while her busy hands braided the reed.

"You could at least clean up the mess," Mrs. Wise said.

"That's my pleasure, my lady," Mr. Gerber said and started indeed to gather everything that was scattered on the floor to put it in big plastic bags.

"It would be nice, if somebody could read a story," Mrs. Raiman suggested.

Everybody looked at Mrs. Pein.

"What about you, Mr. Libarian?" Mrs. Pein asked.

Mr. Guttman blushed and put another piece of wood on the fire. "I am not prepared, but maybe I could find something nice."

The fire crackled and spit sparks. The canary in the background started with a soft voice schiep-schiep-schiep, then it became like a jubilant melody. Mr. Guttman had left and came back shortly after that with a book in his hands. He sat down close to the fire.

"You found something?" Mrs. Pein asked.

"Maybe."

Mrs. Rosenstock looked up. "What's the title of the book?"

"*Stories and more stories*. The eternal Now. It's a fairy tale."

The Eternal Today

Once there was a little girl who lived in a big city with many houses made of stone. In that city there were no trees, only stones and people. But also the hearts of the people were like stone, they all were busy building a wall around themselves. They could not see their neighbour. They lived only for themselves.

The little girl however longed to find a friend. She wanted to find somebody with whom she could share. One day she took a huge ladder and climbed on the upper rung to look beyond the wall. But all she could see was a paved garden without any human being, for here too the people were busy making lots of money to build the wall around their house even higher.

The girl stepped down from the ladder and thought, maybe I have to go where people don't build walls. One day she started on a journey. It lasted hours until she left the city behind. Never before she had left the city, therefore she was surprised to see meadows and fields, even a forest, which made shadows. Around noon the little girl got tired and sat down on a rock that was laying on the way to take a rest. From here the wall that surrounded her city was nothing but a small line on the horizon. But still she did not meet any human being. Were there no living humans anymore, she was wondering. Then she got up to continue her journey. She followed her own shadow, until a cloud covered the sun. Then the child did not know where to go. In the meantime it became evening and the little feet started to hurt, and she felt hungry. She started to cry for she did not know what to do. But nobody was there to comfort her, for there was not a human being around.

In my city there is nobody I could talk to and here is nobody either, she thought. At her right side she saw an old log house. How did this house come to be here in the midst of nowhere? she wondered. and could not remember having seen the house before, even though she had spent a couple of hours in this place. And when the girl looked closer, she saw an old woman sitting at her spinning wheel. She sang a song. A song with a sad melody.

Spindle spin
spindle spin
take the thread and spin
until yesterday and tomorrow
will become today.

These words the old woman repeated again and again and with her foot she stepped the big spinning wheel so quickly that the spokes of the wheel could not be seen anymore. Then the old woman stopped her singsong and the child could only hear the humming of the wheel. Curiously the child came closer.

"What are you doing there?" the girl asked.

Without looking up the old woman said, "I spin the time, until yesterday and tomorrow becomes today."

"Why do you spin the time?" the girl wanted to know.

"Yesterday has passed and tomorrow is not yet, only today. I hold the thread in my hands. But also yesterday had been today and so will tomorrow be. Therefore I am spinning the time so yesterday and tomorrow becomes today. Eternal Now."

"I don't understand this," the child said.

"You can't understand? Why is it that you can't understand? Has your mother never told you about the eternal Now?"

"Mother never talks to me. She does not talk to anybody. Nobody has time to talk to me."

The old woman shook her head in surprise. "It is strange, that nobody talks to you. Don't they talk at all?"

"They do, but not with me."

"What are they talking about?" the old woman wanted to know.

"I don't know. About money and their vacation and cars and food and what they want to do later."

Again the old women shook her head. "And they don't talk with you?"

"Maybe they think I wouldn't understand."

"How old are you?"

"Six."

"Six years. That is much more than two thousand todays. Can you imagine that?"

The girl shook her head. "No."

At that moment the thread broke.

"What are you doing now?" the little one asked.

"I take a piece from yesterday and one piece from tomorrow and spin it together so it becomes Today. And that will be even stronger than before."

"Does it not make a hole in the time?" the child wanted to know.

"Sometimes there is a hole, but only if the thread is not spun. Do you see the wool there in the basket? That all waits to be spun. But if I take it - like that - then it becomes a long thread." The old

woman took the wool and rolled the parts together. "That's how our time is like the people. This all has to come together to become one piece. And one day there comes the time that all threads are spun. Then there will be no more time. Then yesterday and tomorrow will be eternal today. "

"When will that be?"

The old woman shook her shoulders. "That I don't know. That I don't need to know. The important thing is, that I continue to spin."

Mr. Guttman closed the book and put another log on the fire. Nobody said anything. One could only hear the crackling of the fire. Finally Mrs. Pein said, "Maybe that's so. Either we are living in the past with our thoughts or busy with tomorrow and we forget to live today."

"The story should go on. I don't like it, if a story just ends. Then I somehow feel left alone, yes, left alone," Mrs. Wise said.

"Why?" Mr. Guttman wanted to know, "that's the reason for such a story, so everybody can finish it his or her own way. Who always lives in the past or is afraid of tomorrow he is not capable to live today as he is supposed to live. A child lives in the present. It lives now. So it grows. But what it misses today can never be recovered. It is gone. For the wheel turns so quickly, we can hardly see it."

"But what does it have to do with the wall?" Mrs. Wise wanted to know.

"All the threads are connected with each other. Everybody spins his or her own thread, without knowing, but these threads exists of many threads that are woven together. Only then they can make a strong rope."

"I don't know, sometimes I am afraid, my thread could break. What then is left I only imagine. What happens if the thread breaks?"

"A hole," Miss Winter said.

"And that is what I am afraid of."

"But in the story the thread is being spun. There yesterday and tomorrow becomes today," Mr. Guttman said.

"I think the story not only speaks about the past and future and present, it means that the future is already present in today," Mrs. Rosenstock said. "What is time? A splinter from eternity and then going back to eternity again."

"Maybe that is why old people live in the past, they think they don't have a future any more That's a kind of escape," Mrs. Raiman said.

"So we have to help each other to keep the bigger picture in mind," Mrs. Rosenstock said in a low voice.

"And part of that is to tear down the wall, that separates us from our neighbour," Mrs. Pein added. "And I guess we started doing that already, since we are coming together."

"I will miss these evenings," Mrs. Wise admitted.

"Who said that this could not go on even after Christmas?" Mrs. Pein asked.

A home coming

Mrs. Pein was surprised when Mrs. Liebreich called her to her office. She realized that her heart started to pound more quickly and was wondering what she did wrong this time. But as much as she thought, she could not find any wrongdoing. To the contrary, she tried to avoid Mrs. Liebreich as much as possible. Maybe she did not approve of the meetings in the evenings, or the Christmas decorations everywhere? Even on the heavy oak door in the entrance was a wreath hanging with pine cones and stars. Only now she realized that she forgot to ask for permission. This all seemed to be so obvious, that she did not think about it, just did it. Maybe that was it. Mrs. Pein felt like a school girl again being afraid of punishment. "Perhaps we never grow up, no matter how old we are," she thought.

Mrs. Liebreich wore a long jeans skirt buttoned in the front with a white sporty blouse. In the décolletté a pearl necklace could be seen. This time she wore silvery hangers instead of the big ear rings. Mrs. Pein was just thinking what to say as an excuse, when she heard her voice.

"I called you, it's because of the single bed room."

Mrs. Pein took a deep breath of relief. "Is one free?" she asked full of hope.

"You can move in tomorrow."

"Thank you very much! I appreciate this."

"That's the one thing. Now something else. Miss Baumgarten wrote us a letter. She would like to move back to her old room."

"I am glad that she is coming back. But what does it has to do with me?"

"She does not only want her old room back, but she asked that you would be her room mate."

Mrs. Pein realized that her throat became dry. "Did she write that?"

"Here, you can read it yourself." Mrs. Liebreich gave her the letter. Mrs. Pein glanced over the letter and gave it back.

"How long will the single room be available?"

"In case you would agree to stay where you are, we would transfer Mrs. Long, your present room mate, instead."

"Would it not be better, if Miss Baumgarten would take the single room?"

"That is what I thought too, but we can't let her be on her own. It would be better if somebody is around all the time, in case something happens."

"I understand."

Mrs. Pein looked outside the window. The sky was like a grey metal plate.

"You don't need to make a decision right away, you can tell me tomorrow morning."

Suddenly the first encounter came back to her mind. Could she cope with all that again? The noise of the television, the light, the quarrel. She did not feel strong enough. But what should she do?

"It's because of the television, you know. To be honest, the biggest problem is the noise of the television. I hardly ever look myself."

"We could put the television into the lounge."

"This would be a solution, but what would Miss Baumgarten say?"

"I think we can talk about this very honestly. We can tell her, that she can't have both, you and the television. Then she can decide. But as I can see this would not be a question for her."

The day before Christmas Miss Baumgarten returned from the hospital. A huge ribbon was dangling from one end to the next in the entrance hall. *Welcome back* was written in large letters. Toni and Hanna Venicetti had fastened the banner and Mrs. Liebreich did not object.

"Only the band from the Salvation Army is missing," she said half mockingly.

Two men from the ambulance accompanied Miss Baumgarten to her room. Nothing was changed. Only there where there had been a television before now stood a comfortable armchair. Miss Baumgarten looked around, her eyes widened, when she saw the Christmas decoration.

"It looks different," she said and started to unpack her suitcase. "It's good to be back again. I tell you, that's not life over there. Always on a plate, no privacy. I hate that feeling, you are so powerless. Others are in control over your life. I really hate that feeling. This is still my body and as long as I am breathing, I want to be in charge. But it does not work that way. I am a nobody. Others tell me what to do. I have to swallow whatever they put in my mouth. And if I ask what it is, they get grumpy. No, I tell you, that's no life. Glad to be back."

"Good to have you back. We really missed you."

"You really did? Nobody ever missed me."

"Aunt Pein!" a high child's voice could be heard outside the door.

Mrs. Pein opened. At the door was Helena with a huge basket of fruit.

"My Mom sent this. There are also some cookies. I baked them myself, for the lady from the hospital."

"Come in, Helena, I have to introduce you to my old friend Miss Baumgarten. She does not know you yet."

Helena looked a bit timid.

"That's my little friend Helena," Mrs. Pein explained. "She lives here."

Miss Baumgarten shook her head. "Here? In our home? What you don't say. No, I don't believe it. Mrs. Liebreich would never allow that."

"Her father is our new cook, and her mother will work here as well in the beginning of next year."

"For tonight my Mom has a surprise for you, but I am not supposed to tell."

"Is that so?" Then she turned to Miss Baumgarten, "things have changed here. If you would like to know and you are not too tired, I could take you along to our Gingerbread House I have told you about."

Miss Baumgarten closed the suitcase and put it into the storage room. Then she sat down in the armchair and looked again.

"I can't believe it. That I am back again - - it's a miracle. What do you mean Gingerbread House?

"You forgot? I told you about it. I'll show you later tonight."

But that did not happen. When they opened the door to the dining hall Christmas songs sounded from a tape recorder. The tables were arranged differently, this time not as a horseshoe but in little groups. Each table with a red tablecloth and a burning candle and an arrangement with pine needles. The old people were standing there and did not know what to say. Some of them started to cry, others secretly wiped their wet eyes. Miss Baumgarten sat beside Mrs. Pein.

"Something like that had never happened as long as I was here. I would like to know what - - " she stopped talking for at that moment a choir started to sing "Holy night." Helena's bright voice suddenly stopped, so her mother continued the song, now again Helena sang and always looked at Mrs. Pein. Her eyes glistened. Mrs. Pein waved back, then at the second verse some voices fell in. One after another stood up and tuned in as good as they could. Then other songs followed. Mr. Guttman read the Christmas story. Then there was a pause. Mrs. Venicetti gave a signal to the girls, that were waiting, and immediately they started to go from one table to the next. Each young lady had a white apron and a white hair band. The food smelled very tasty. Even the potato balls were decorated and the roast was served on big plates along with salad and cheese.

"Never could I have guessed something like this!" Miss Baumgarten could not believe such change. Everybody could see how glad she was to be back again.

"For desert we have another surprise!" Mrs. Venicetti said.

"It's nothing special, just a little thank you for your warm welcome," Mr. Venicetti added.

"Who is that?" Miss Baumgarten asked in a whisper.

"Mr. Venicetti, the cook." And while Mrs. Pein briefly explained, she could see that the belly of Mrs. Venicetti showed a slight bulge.

"I can't believe it, now we soon will have a new family member!" Mrs. Pein thought.

Helena sprang up and down for excitement and clapped her hands. The door opened and a real Santa Claus came in with a red coat and a long white beard, and beside him his helper with a huge sack and a stick.

The old people started to laugh, some of them laughed so loudly that their laughter was contagious. One could hardly understand what Santa Claus was saying. Mrs. Liebreich entered unnoticed and remained standing at the door.

Santa Claus opened his huge sack and fetched the first parcel out of it, then the second one. He read one name after the next and as soon as the one showed his or her hand, Helena came running to deliver the little parcel.

"This voice sounds so familiar," Mrs. Pein murmured, "if only I would know!" Suddenly she knew: Mr. Walther, Jan's brother Charles. Then the helper could be nobody else than Jan. Now Mrs. Pein got her parcel. It was a book. She knew that right away. Carefully she unwrapped the Christmas paper and read, *Stories and even more stories* Volume II. Next Miss Baumgarten got her parcel.

"I can't believe it!" She said again and again and stroked lovingly over the beautiful wrapping.

"Mrs. Liebreich!" Santa Claus read and looked around. No hand was raised. Helena pointed to Mrs. Liebreich who was still standing at the door, took the parcel and ran to the door to hand it over to Mrs. Liebreich. She took it and went behind the counter. When Santa Claus and his helper were about to leave, Toni protested.

"You can't do that to us! You have to stay here and share the meal!" Santa Claus pointed to his long beard and said, "That would be too difficult," and his helper nodded. "We still have work to do." With that they waved good-bye.

Suddenly Mrs. Pein remembered the teddy. She got up and hurried out of the dining room. She could see neither Santa Claus nor his helper any more. Mrs. Pein went into her room and got the teddy out of the wardrobe. Helena was sitting beside her parents at a separate table.

"Santa Claus forgot something," Mrs. Pein said and put the teddy into the little child's arms.

Helena jumped up. "Mom, a real teddy, look!". With that she embraced Mrs. Pein with all her strength, so she nearly fell, if Toni had not held her.

"Not that hard, my daughter!" he said laughingly and raised his finger.

In the meantime it was seven o'clock and still nobody wanted to leave.

"Today we will forget about the Gingerbread House," Mrs. Pein said to Miss Baumgarten. It can wait. In a couple of days everything will be pulled down again."

Back to everyday life

When Christmas was over suddenly there was a void. All the effort and hassle had come to an end. What next? They had gotten to know each other. The common goal brought them closer. But what should happen next?

"Too bad it's over," Mrs. Wise said.

"There is not Christmas all-year-round," Mrs. Long said. During all these days she did not mention once her Dodo. And Mrs. Pein did not want to ask.

"I never thought, that we would sell that much!" Mrs. Pein said.

"We even could have sold more!" Mrs. Wise said self-confidently.

"But so far we don't know what to do with all the money." That was the voice of Mr. Guttman.

While he was talking, Miss Zundel came. She had not come to any of the meetings yet. Her face was inscrutable. This time she did not wear make-up, therefore her lines appeared even deeper. When she saw all the people she asked partly curiously, partly irritated,

"What happened?"

"We are just talking about the past couple of weeks," Mrs. Pein explained.

Miss Zundel made a devaluated gesture. "I'm glad that everything is over. That's not for me. It's just a show, nothing else. A big self-deception, that's what it is."

"What do you mean?" Mrs. Pein asked somehow helpless.

"Why are you celebrating? To lift the mood, that's all. You are lying to yourself."

The atmosphere changed immediately. How could it be that one negative comment could influence the whole atmosphere?

"Don't you believe that God sent the Messiah?"

Miss Zundel shook her shoulders disdainfully. "Old wives stories."

"Without Him everything would be indeed hopeless," Mrs. Pein said. At that very moment she remembered that Miss Zundel had lost all her family through a terrorist attack. "There are scars in our lives that will stay with us for ever, but this does not mean that we have to hurt others in return."

"We got side-tracked from our subject," Mr. Guttman said, "What about an outing by bus and staying overnight somewhere?"

"In winter?" Miss Bremer asked doubtfully.

"This can be very beautiful, and if there is still money left, we could repeat such an adventure in spring."

"I am afraid that our money would not be enough for that. Imagine the costs of one stay in a hotel!" Mr. Gerber warned.

"My brother-in-law owns a travel business. I could ask him if he could provide a bus with driver for free."

"That would be wonderful, Mrs. Raiman!" Mrs. Pein got excited.

"And where to?"

"Somewhere to the mountains," Mr. Gerber suggested.

"Preferable to a lake," was the wish of Mrs. Wise.

"By chance does somebody have a brother-in-law who owns a hotel at a lake?"

They all laughed.

"You won't believe it, but we made so much money that it would cover two nights," Mr. Guttman said.

"What if we stay for one night and the rest of the money we donate to something special? There is so much need around us," Mrs. Rosenstock asked.

"Does anybody have an idea?" Mr. Guttman hastened to ask.

"My daughter is a teacher for handicapped children. Sometimes she talks about those kids. Often they are experiencing a terrible life. They are humans like you and me. I often wished I could help," said Mrs. Rosenstock.

"Could your daughter tell us something about her job?" Mrs. Pein asked.

"I am sure, she would love to do that."

Mrs. Long rummaged in her handbag and searched for her lipstick, then she took out a small mirror and started to paint her lips. "Miss Zundel is right, what's that all about. What do you expect from all that? Such an event does not make a difference, it won't make a dent into your dull life. We are on a siding." She put back her lipstick, took the powder-box out, but immediately closed it again.

"If you have the impression you are on a siding, then it's time to rearrange the switch," Mrs. Pein said.

"It's a terminus with no way out. The cemetery is right across the street, so it's not too far to go for relatives," Mrs. Long continued and opened once more her powder-box and dabbed her cheeks. Then she put it back and closed the bag with a click.

Nobody said a word, but everybody could sense how a dark cloud hovered over the room.

"Getting old often comes along with pain," Mrs. Rosenstock said. "But those pains are like the pangs of a new life. It's not important how the child is being born, what is important is that it comes to life. Sometimes I have the impression a new being grows deep within us, and one day it steps out into life. And all the pain we are suffering belongs to our life. It would not be good to fight against it."

"You can say that easily. But look at me? I have arthritis. Do you know how that is?" Miss Zundel showed her crooked fingers. "I can't do anything without pain."

"Maybe you would forget your pain through such a kind of event," Mr. Guttman said.

"Forget! That only shows that you have no idea! I prefer to stay where I am. To travel around, that is not for me."

"That may be," Mrs. Pein said. "But the older we get, the less mobile we are. It's a real danger that we stay where we were and just let life pass by. This is not good. The border gets narrower from year to year. What we can do becomes less with every year. There is more and more we can't do any longer. It costs effort to enlarge these boundary-poles. Do you want to suffocate? It's important to stay mobile, not only inside, also from the outside. My father sometimes told me about an old farmer who was handicapped due to an accident. Together with his son he trained day by day, everyday the poles were pushed out meter by meter. One meter did not make a big difference, but in the course of a year this was quite a distance! And at the end of the year he could assume the old job again. If he had given up, he would not gained anything." Mrs. Pein looked up and asked: "Did I tell you this story once before?"

"Once?" Mrs. Raiman laughed, "at least ten times! But it's necessary to hear it again and again."

That shows how important it became to me. I never forgot it."

"It doesn't mean anything to me," Miss Zundel said.

"I can imagine that your situation is not nice," Mrs. Pein said.

"Not nice?"

"I mean it's difficult for you, but in spite of that - - "

"Have you been there? Have you?"

"No."

"Then you better shut up."

"But - - "

"Then you don't understand."

"Do you mean we should withdraw?" Mrs. Pein asked. Suddenly the first day in the home came to her mind, when she entered the dining hall and got the impression as if she would suffocate. Even then she realized how negative Miss Zundel was. Could it be that there was nothing that could help her to come out of this attitude? "We need each other. You need us and we need you. If one of us can't see any more, then there is somebody else who becomes the eye. If somebody can't hear any more, then somebody else comes along to lend him his ear. The same with our feet. Who can't walk, somebody else comes along to help. That's how we grow together. I guess, the older we get, the more we are aware of that. You know, I am not a master of words. This is not my talent. Never was. The thoughts, they just come out, before I am able to catch them. I can talk with my heart more than with my mouth. But I know that with your anger you are poisoning the atmosphere and you don't help anyone with that."

"You are preaching like a pastor in church," Miss Zundel said and got up.

Mrs. Pein was silent. Miss Zundel looked at Mrs. Pein somehow guilty. "I did not want to hurt you."

There was an embarrassing silence. Nobody really knew what to say. Finally Mrs. Pein said, "You are angry. This I can understand. Sometimes I too am looking for someone I could make responsible for my situation. That is how we humans react. We are angry about those who have a better life than we, we are angry with God, who does not help, we are angry about ourselves because we are so helpless. That's how it is. But with our anger we only harm ourselves."

"There you are again preaching!" This time it was Mrs. Long, who came to rescue Miss Zundel.

"I only say what I see. Can you improve a situation through your anger? No. It only gets worse. And we isolate ourselves."

"That's the way I am," Miss Zundel said bitterly.

"That's your justification."

Suddenly there was a shrill noise. "Oh sorry, my hearing-aid," Mrs. Wise lifted her arm, to regulate her hearing-aid. The high beeping stopped. "I still have to get used to it," she said and laughed. "Sometimes it's quite annoying, but we are among ourselves."

Miss Zundel left. "Then enjoy."

Also Mrs. Long got up. Others remained seated. Mrs. Pein turned to Miss Baumgarten, who had not said a word all evening.

"Would you come along when we go?"

"What do you think! Do you think I would stay here? I take another Aspirin, but something like that I don't want to miss."

They were now in a small circle. The fire place showed only a faint glimmer. Miss Winter got up and sat down on an empty chair, where Miss Zundel sat before. One could see that she wanted to say something.

"When I came here, I thought, that's the last stretch. After that there is nothing. That's the end. Over. And I had waited year after year for that moment when I could start to live. That day was always in the future, somewhere far away. Then I thought, as soon as I am married, I have time to think about myself and do what is pleasing me. But soon the children came. Then I thought, as soon as the children are grown up and left the house, my time has come. But then came the grandchildren. Then it was sickness. Then I was old. And now I don't have time to start something new."

"Did you not say that you did pottery when you were young?" Mrs. Pein asked.

"That's true, but that's long time ago. This was nothing special."

"Often we count what we do for nothing, only what others are doing seems to be big in our eyes."

"Maybe, maybe that's so. But now I have the feeling to have reached the end. That's my problem."

"Nobody knows how much time is left. It could well be that you will survive all of us. Who knows. What is important is that we seize the time that is given to us," Mr. Guttman thrust in.

"I can understand what Miss Winter said," Mrs. Raiman said. "It's this daily routine, the everyday stuff without any highlight. There is nothing special happening."

"Then we have to create these special events!"

Miss Winter looked hopeless. "But what if we have reached the peak already and are on our way down? There is nothing we are looking forward to. Nothing worthwhile to fight for. No goal to reach."

"Then it's time to enjoy the rest and peace of silence, that we learn to see the beauty around us and find our satisfaction somewhere else," Mrs. Rosenstock said.

"And if you lost your sight?"

"There are new worlds deep inside we have to open up."

"I believe, Mrs. Rosenstock is right. When the privilege of a young person is activity, the advantage of the old people the reflection and peace of mind, the being." Mrs. Pein said.

"That all sounds nice. But to be - how do you do that?"

"You can't make it, it is there," Mrs. Rosenstock tried to explain.

"That is all? I don't know, somehow I want to start from the beginning, start life again."

When Miss Winter said that, it was as if they all held their breath. Was it not what they all thought sometimes?

"I feel cheated by life. And then the feeling of not being able to start anew, that causes something in me - I just can't describe it."

"That's it. I too would like to go back, just to have another chance, but I can't," Mrs. Raiman said.

"You know, if this life would be all there is, then indeed it would be enough to drive one to despair," Mrs. Rosenstock now threw in, "but the real life is still ahead of us. This life here is just a preparation. Sometimes it's an easy introduction, sometimes it can be dramatic. But it's only a passage."

Now Mr. Muller left as well. For a while nobody talked. Then Mrs. Rosenstock continued, "Also the darkness belongs to life. That is the mystery of evil, that is hidden. Everything has two sides. And where there is evil, there is good as well."

Mr. Guttman nodded: "We humans too have two sides as well, the right and left."

Mr. Gerber sat erect and cleared his throat. "And what about our head? I have only one!" he said triumphantly.

"That's true, but our brain has two parts, the right and the left," Mr. Guttman said.

"These two sides belong together, only then we are whole."

"That's true, we also have two eyes and two ears, two arms and hands and legs."

Mrs. Wise was surprised, "I never thought about it!"

"But only one nose." Mr. Gerber said nearly stubbornly.

Mr. Guttman laughed, "with two openings."

Mr. Gerber did not want to give in. "But only one mouth!"

"And this mouth has two parts as well, the upper jaw and the lower one," Mr. Guttman replied.

They all laughed and for a moment they forgot that they were not children anymore.

"These two parts belong together like day and night, being awake and sleeping, like joy and sadness, laughter and crying, life and death. That's our life," Mrs. Rosenstock said.

"Do you mean that evil belongs to life as well?" Mrs. Raiman was wondering.

"Maybe. Maybe they pollinate each other. Only we can't see it."

"And what about sickness?" Miss Baumgarten asked, who was following the conversation with great interest, but did not participate so far.

"Sickness is striving for health again, the other side, where the seed bears fruit. You believe in eternity, do you? You know, I believe, it's like Mrs. Pein said, this all belongs to the same picture. Also evil belongs to giving birth, like birth pangs that bring forth new life. Sometimes it hurts badly. Then we think we cannot take it any longer, we cry and want to die - but then new life comes through. And when we are holding this new vulnerable life in our arms, it's a miracle. Good and perfect."

"But what about a miscarriage?" That was Miss Bremer.

"Yes, there are congenital defects, that too is a mystery. One of my daughters has a handicapped child. It has down syndrome. At first it was extremely difficult for all of us, we just could not accept it. We had longed for a healthy child. But it was not to be. 'The mystery is with God', my father said. We are living here in a dark room where the picture is being developed. But God is our master. Something good will come out of it, that's for sure."

That was the end of the conversation.

The trip

The rain poured down. For hours the bus followed the seemingly endless bending street. The driver changed the gear. The heavy vehicle was pushing up the mountain. The windows were clouded, one could hardly look outside. Mrs. Pein tried to clear the window pane with her sleeves. The thick rain wall did not allow her to look through. She could not even see the mountains. She put her forehead against the glass and could sense the vibration of the motor. Miss Baumgarten sat beside her and slept.

"I told you we should stay home. That's nothing for me. Rain I can have at home, for that I don't need to go out," Mrs. Pein heard a voice complaining from behind and turned around. She already knew this nagging voice. It was Miss Zundel.

Mrs. Pein became angry. "It always depends what we are doing in a certain situation."

"Doing - what could we do? To stop the rain?" Miss Zundel asked snappishly.

The bus started to sway

"If that continues I will get seasick," she said reproachfully. "Going on a trip at such a season!"

They had all come along, except Mr. Muller, who was transferred the day before into another home and Mrs. Long, who was invited by her daughter over the weekend. Otherwise they all came along. Mrs. Pein was surprised when she saw them all together in the entrance hall waiting. The evening before they had a heavy discussion. Somebody suggested to pay the trip for the handicapped children through a special offering. Miss Zundel was strictly against it. She argued that the trip already cost more than she could afford and she was not willing to pay in addition, not even one penny. When Mr. Guttman at the end of the meeting counted the money, there were many ten dollar notes, even one fifty dollar note and one hundred. Together with the money from the Gingerbread House bazaar it was enough not only to pay for their own expenses, but also for the nine children and their teacher!

Suddenly they all heard from the front row a woman's voice: "One-two-three" - and at the same moment high children voices sounded through the bus and woke up the sleepers even in the last row. Then they clapped the rhythm with their hands. Tired heads were raised to see the children. Even Miss Baumgarten looked up.

"How can somebody sing in such weather?" Miss Zundel hissed.

Mrs. Pein tried to understand what they were singing, but she could not find out. Only some words she could make out. Deborah Anderson was sitting in the midst of her children.

"We want to sing a song for you all, it's very simple, and after that we can sing it all together. The words are:

Look at the mountain
forget all your pain
the rain makes us happy
let's all cry: yippee

She started with her high soprano and clapped the time. The children sang with all their might.

"Let's try together! The children will sing once more and you can try to join in!"

"That's silly," Miss Zundel grumbled. "Just silly!"

"Let's try - together:
Look at the mountain
forget all your pain....

At first the clapping would not come easily, but the second time, it was much better.

"Again!" Deborah Anderson cried, and the children sang even louder:

"Look at the mouun-tain
forget all your paaain - -"

When the last tone ebbed Mrs. Pein clapped her hands. Heads turned in amazement. She continued to clap.

"Do you have another song?" she called through the bus.

Deborah Anderson thought for a moment. "We have plenty!"

"Ju-hutsch", one of the children suggested.

"That's good! Again the text is very simple:

Can't see the sun,
just get higher
ju-hutsch
still you can't see?
just get higher
ju-hutsch!
ju-hutsch. ju-hutsch,. ju-hutsch!"

With this the children stretched high their arms, then clapped their hands three times.

Now even the last person was awake. Miss Zundel got impatient. "How long does it still take?"

Mr. Guttman turned to Mrs. Rosenstock, who sat beside him, "What a blessing these children!"

Mrs. Rosenstock nodded. "Deborah knows how to talk to them. She loves them with all her heart."

"I should have brought Jan along," Mrs. Pein thought, "he would have enjoyed it very much." But this thought had not crossed her mind. "Next time, if we are going again, I will ask him to come along," and once more she wiped with her sleeves the moisture from the window. Suddenly there was a fascinating view. Apparently they climbed the pass through the clouds. The valley stretched deep down. Thick clouds pushed along the cliffs. Now the sun broke through and painted a colourful rainbow from one end to the next, as if embracing the whole valley. The bus came to a halt.

"We will have a rest for twenty minutes," the bus driver announced. "If anyone wants to drink coffee, there is an opportunity to do so."

One after another left the bus.

"Too cold outside," Miss Zundel lamented, "I'll catch a cold. I should have stayed at home, there at least I have my television."

Nobody paid any attention to her. Miss Zundel realizing that she was the only one left in the bus, got up, however remained on the last step of the bus. Then she discovered the restaurant and stepped out.

Little Jonathan came running to his grandmother. When he saw Miss Zundel, he was frightened and looked at her with wide open eyes. Then he said, so everybody could hear, "Grandma, this lady has a mouth like a rainbow, only not as colourful!"

"Jonathan," Mrs. Rosenstock said appalled and bowed down to him.

"Don't say something like that," she whispered. "You don't know her. Perhaps something is hurting her."

"Why doesn't she sing Ju-hutsch?"

Mrs. Rosenstock took the little one in her arms, "That's not always that easy, darling."

Jonathan jumped up and down and cried as loud as he could: "Ju-hutsch, ju-hutsch. ju-hutsch!"

"Jonathan!" Deborah Anderson called alarmed.

Mrs. Pein saw how much Deborah resembled her mother. The delicate profile, the dark eyes, only the hair was still black and reached over her shoulders. On her face lay a soft sadness, which she often saw in Mrs. Rosenstock. Mrs. Pein was standing at the low wall that separated the parking place from a grassy place. The restaurant stuck to a rock wall like an eagle's nest. Deep down in the valley she could see a lake. Its green colour fascinated her. She could recognise several white dots. Could it be that somebody was out there with his sail boat? Now Miss Baumgarten joined her.

"Finally it stopped raining. It was long enough!"

"The soil smells, the air is so clean up here." Mrs. Pein took a deep breath. She could hardly see the rainbow anymore. It slowly faded away.

"Shall we go inside for a cup of coffee? That would warm us from the inside."

"You can go, I prefer to stay here. The view is fantastic, like a fairy tale. Can you see this panorama? So many peaks woven together, and every one has its own shadow. What a great artist who has designed all this! And the sky!" Mrs. Pein could hardly take in all the beauty.

"It's hard to imagine that on this planet there is so much suffering," Miss Baumgarten said. "Such injustice, lies, greed, sickness, disappointment, death. All that!"

"But there is the other side as well," Mrs. Pein said.

"And this world rests on four pillars: Justice, truth, love and mercy," Mrs. Rosenstock added who just joined the two, then turned away.

"I wish we would have a bit more of that," Miss Baumgarten said and left to go to the restaurant.

The sun glittered in a silvery band, that was winding through the valley.

"It's a long time since I have been to the mountains. I really looked forward to this. The seemingly endless beauty where you can forget all suffering. I am glad that we drove in spite of all the rain," Mrs. Pein said and suddenly realized that she was talking to herself. Miss Baumgarten had left for the restaurant. Then Mrs. Pein saw Mrs. Rosenstock as she was leaning against the low wall.

"You have a beautiful daughter," she said.

"Yes, that's true. And I am very proud of her."

"She knows how to handle those kids."

"I am often surprised myself what she does. You can hardly see that they are not normal kids."

"I guess, it always depends how you approach them."

"There they are coming", Mrs. Rosenstock pointed down to the steep stony way that was winding up the slope.

"I would be afraid one of them would slip and fall."

"They are used to it."

"Look, isn't this Mr. Guttman?"

"Yes, Jonathan found a friend."

"A nice person, this Mr. Guttman, don't you think so?"

"What do you know about him?" Mrs. Rosenstock asked quickly.

"I've known him from years back in the library. He often helped me find something. I always admired his knowledge and friendliness. He was interested in so many subjects, it was always a pleasure to talk with him."

"We have many things in common," Mrs. Rosenstock said.

"This you can't find so often."

Mrs. Rosenstock was silent.

"Did he talk about the concert?"

Mrs. Rosenstock made a defensive gesture. "I don't know."

"He told me, you are an excellent pianist."

"He exaggerates."

"I am not so sure about that. Won't you try?"

"After so many years?"

"Just for us."

"That's what Mr. Guttman said. He insisted." She laughed. "Another new characteristic, just like my late husband."

"He loves music, especially the classic."

"That's true. The love of music always brings people together." Mrs. Pein stated. Did she say too much? She did not want to appear too intrusive and changed the subject.

In the west again dark clouds formed. Slowly the bus filled up. Everybody took their place. The people felt refreshed and were happily talking with each other. The bus carefully drove higher, still higher. The first drops were hammering against the window and turned into crooked little streams. Suddenly the rain became snow. Thick flakes whirled around and covered the window with a white layer like icing. Around ten o'clock in the evening they reached their destination. The bright moonlight fell on the snowy pathway. The house resembled a little castle with alcoves and turrets. Apparently they were expected, somebody must have seen them coming, for by and by little lamps were lit and showed the way. The snow was piled at both sides.

Mr. Guttman carried one of the sleeping little ones on his shoulders, also Mr. Gerber was holding one child in his arms. Little Jonathan was still asleep in the lap of Mrs. Raiman, who was driving her electric wheelchair. In the roomy entrance hall a fire was flickering in the fire place and sent a pleasant warmth. The flames reflected on the dark beams At the windows comfortable armchairs with dark covers were arranged. From somewhere came soft music. A friendly lady in her mid fifties greeted the new comers.

"I am Renate Berger and welcome you in the name of the house. I hope you will enjoy your stay with us. We will try to make your stay as pleasant as possible. If somebody would like something to eat or to drink, our restaurant is open until eleven o'clock."

Through a large glass door they could see the restaurant with nicely decorated tables and red serviettes and glasses and in the middle of each table a little candle, sending a warm light.

"Breakfast is between 8 and 9, also in the restaurant. If you have any questions, we are here for you."

Now Miss Berger turned to Mrs. Raiman who was waiting in her wheelchair, "Are you Mrs. Raiman? We have a room for you on the first floor. One of our girls will lead you there. Telephone is in your room."

Deborah took the sleeping child from Mrs. Raiman's lap to free her way. Miss Berger rang a little bell on top of the counter and immediately several helpers came to lead everybody to their rooms.

Everything was prepared. Each room had it's own bath and toilet and a view on the lake - but now it was dark and they could not see the lake. Deborah Anderson and her children were all sleeping on the floor in a large hall in the attic.

Mrs. Pein put her bag on the floor. She could not believe how cosy everything was. The bed was big and covert with a colourful bedspread. Beside the bed was a night table with a lamp and telephone. On the wall opposite the bed a desk with another lamp and to her right a comfortable armchair. The room was much more roomy than her own in the home, and so much more attractive! The television was placed on a low commode with some drawers. At the wall there was a painting with a wooden frame. Immediately she recognised that it was Van Gogh's *Harvest*. She just loved this idyllic village image with its warm colours. She opened the door to the bathroom and was surprised to find an elegant bath and a shelf with towels. On top of the basin was a little basket with bath utensils like soap, shower cap and shampoo. She took off her shoes and enjoyed the softness of the carpet. She stepped to the window and pulled back the soft curtain. At that moment the moon broke through the dark clouds, reflecting in the water. She opened the window to breathe in the fresh mountain air. She could hear the rustling of the trees. How could she sleep in midst of such beauty! And again she regretted that she did not take Jan with her. Surely he had never seen something like that. Suddenly the sky was clear. She turned off the light. Slowly the stars came out, one after another, and soon the sky was over sown with glittering stars. She had never seen the stars that close. Maybe once, when her husband was still alive.

She undressed herself and lay down on her bed and listened to the silence.

The next morning she was awakened by the rays of the sun. The sky stretched in a glowing blue over the mountain lake. Waterfowls circled the rock with loud voices and settled down on the top, but shortly after that they again raised their heavy wings and sailed in even slaps over the water.

Mrs. Pein went into the bath room and dressed herself. She looked into the mirror and was thinking about Mrs. Liebreich. This would be good for her, she thought. We should have taken her along, but nobody would have felt comfortable in her company. This would have caused others not to come. And she was wondering, how could it be that one person has such an emanation.

When she entered the restaurant most of the guests were already waiting. The pleasant smell of coffee greeted her. In a small basket were fresh baked rolls. Mrs. Pein got a seat at the window, facing the park. The gnarled old trees were covered with a layer of snow. Through the branches she could see the clear dark blue of the sky. Even the benches were covered with a white cap. "Like Toni in the kitchen," she thought. She had asked the family to come along, but Hanna Venicetti was afraid of the long drive in her expecting stage. What should happen if she had to give birth on the way? Even though she knew that the house was well equipped and a helicopter could land on the roof to bring her into a hospital - there was still a danger involved.

A young friendly girl went from one table to the next to serve the guests.

"Guess who comes here!" one of the girls called out with a happy voice, "my little friends!"

Mrs. Pein turned around and saw Deborah Anderson coming with the children.

"Did you all sleep well?" The girl asked and showed them their place. For them a special niche was reserved with long cushioned benches. The high backs of the benches served as flowerpots with lush green hanging plants. The chatting of the children drowned the background music.

Deborah Anderson waved towards Mrs. Pein and pointed to the children. "It's time that they roam around outside!"

"Could you find sleep at all?"

"They slept through."

"And what about you?"

She laughed. "Not much. Maybe I don't need as much any more. It's like a dream up here. I had not expected that!"

When the young server reached the table again, Mrs. Pein asked, "Is it slippery outside?"

"The way to the shore is cleared."

Mrs. Pein thought about the walker and the wheelchair.

"Don't worry, we have some special cars for handicapped people," the young lady said. "The folks at the desk are prepared. We often have groups of handicapped people."

When Ms Pein looked by chance to her right, she saw Miss Zundel. She held her mirror and played with her lips, trying to pull them up. This was so funny that Mrs. Pein hardly could suppress laughing. Then she remembered how little Jonathan compared her mouth with a rainbow. Maybe this spontaneous observation of a handicapped child gave her a lesson. Suddenly Miss Zundel felt watched and quickly put back the mirror.

Even though it was mid January the sun was strong already and warmed the air. However, the wind blew that they could hardly fight against it.

Fascinated the old people were standing at the lake and watching the play of the waves, that were splashing against the rocky shore. The children could hardly be tamed. With loud squeaking they ran towards the water, but stopped just in front of it.

Then they started to roll over in the snow. At first Mrs. Pein was shocked, but then she realized that it was the pure joy of life. It was impossible for Deborah Anderson to control all the children at once. Her cheeks were glowing, the dark strands of hair were blown around her face. On each hand she was holding one child. Mr. Guttman and Mrs. Rosenstock tried to help her, and so was Mr. Gerber, who was holding a child. Everyone who felt strong enough took over responsibility for one child. This was not organized, it came spontaneously. Only those of the old people who were afraid remained in the special car and were driving slowly along the lake.

"Bum-bum!" a little boy said pointing with his tiny bulky hands to the water. Mrs. Pein constantly watched him, ready to grab him. She felt relieved when she realized that he was too afraid to go closer to the water. As soon as a new wave came, he ran to Mrs. Pein, who embraced him lovingly, but then went back to the water again. Mr. Guttman was totally out of breath. He had two of those who were difficult to tame.

"Enough!" Deborah Anderson called, and again "enough!" But her voice was swallowed by the wind. It took a while until the last child understood that is was time to stop.

Could it be? Mrs. Pein thought she had seen wrong. Miss Zundel was playing with a little girl, that was laughing and her hands clapped for excitement.

Mrs. Pein heard the voice of Miss Zundel: "Da-da-da-da", and saw how she clapped with her crippled hands. Maybe she forgot her pain for a moment, she thought and grabbed the hand of her little pupil.

"What's your name?" Mrs. Pein asked, but the little one did not answer, just wanted to return to the water. But when she saw that Deborah Anderson was already on her way to the hotel, she dragged the child with her.

"We have to go home," she said.

"Don't want to," said the child. "Noooo!" She started to cry. Mrs. Pein felt helpless. She looked around to see if somebody was near who could help. In that moment Deborah Anderson came running and snatched the child and carried her to the vehicle that was waiting. But now all the children wanted to get a ride as well and came running behind the car. Before they knew it they were at the parking place, where the bus was waiting.

A new perspective

From that time on the house guests met at the lounge regularly and talked about various ideas. One of them suggested that they could renovate the gym and start with exercises, others came up with the idea of a concert and theatre evenings, and again somebody else wanted an evening of story telling. Also another trip was planned. Only they could not come to an agreement where to go this time. Some even volunteered for kitchen help. And one room was reserved as a workshop with a real easel, where they all could try their painting skills.

"Mrs. Pein, I thought about it," Jan said to her one day. "My pension is enough to live. I don't need to pay rent. As you know I inherited the property and the workshop. Apart from that, I don't have anything. But I don't need more. Then I thought, maybe I could help somehow. I don't need much, a small room, that's all. It doesn't even need to have running water. In my workshop I don't have water either. If it's warm, that would be good. Warm would be good. What do you think?"

Mrs. Pein looked at him in surprise. "You would - -"

Jan nodded.

"And what did you have in mind?"

"Housekeeper perhaps or gardener or something like that. Something, where I can be on my own. You know, I am not good with people. But totally on my own, that's not good either."

"There is another small house that belongs to this property that's empty. I wanted to talk about it with Mrs. Liebreich a long time ago. Maybe now would be a good opportunity. Everything could be so different but somehow the vision is missing. Yes, I believe there has to be a vision and courage to change old ways," Mrs. Pein said. She only had to wait for the right time.

It was the first of February. The lounge was filled to the last place. They even had to get chairs from the dining hall. Mr. Guttman had planned everything and the tuner had tuned the piano. Now the last tone died away. Mrs. Rosenstock slowly got up. The long black silk dress reached to the floor. She wore a necklace of white plaited pearls. Her wavy white hair glistened. Mr. Guttman got up and applauded. One after the other followed his example. Mrs. Pein watched Mrs. Liebreich during this evening. She sat in the front row. It was the first time that she had ever taken part in an event. The program was still in her hand. Now she put the program aside, got up and applauded as well. Mrs. Rosenstock bowed with grace. Mr. Guttman gave a sign to Helena, who immediately took the huge bouquet of red roses to give them to Mrs. Rosenstock. She smiled somehow shyly and bowed once more. Mr. Guttman was still applauding.

"This was excellent," Mrs. Pein overheard somebody saying. Miss Baumgarten was sitting next to her. "I would never have thought this," she said and in her voice was real admiration. Slowly one after the other left the room. Mrs. Pein was looking for Mrs. Liebreich. She was about to leave the room, when Mrs. Pein talked to her.

"Mrs. Liebreich would you have a minute?"

Mrs. Liebreich looked up in surprise. "Now?"

"If possible?"

"Then come to my office."

While they were on their way to the office, Mrs. Liebreich said, "Chopin was played brilliantly. I know the difference. I had no idea. This lady is world class, and then in our home!"

Mrs. Pein thought she did not hear right. "Something like that I did not expect either," she quickly added. "Too bad that we did not announce it for the public. We should have put an ad in the paper."

"Perhaps next time," Mrs. Liebreich said.

"That's a good idea, such concerts should be given more often."

"The room is too small for that, and the piano. I felt sorry for her. By the way, I was surprised, I could not remember that it was ever tuned."

"This was the responsibility of Mr. Guttman."

"Who paid for that?"

"We all did."

They had reached the office. "I won't allow that. That's the duty of the house. Just give me the bill and I will pay for that." Mrs. Liebreich sat down and invited Mrs. Pein to do the same. "I seldom heard Chopin being played that way. I was really impressed."

"You know, these years could become the best ever for these people. Most of them had a difficult life. They are frustrated and disappointed."

Suddenly it was as if Mrs. Liebreich would fall back into her old self again.

"Do you expect me to make allowance for that?"

"Surely not, but you could contribute so this time becomes the climax of their lives."

"I don't know what you want. I am not interested in other people's lives. I have enough as it is with my own. Everybody has to take responsibility for his own life, that's what my mother always said."

"That does not mean it is right. We are responsible for each other. We can't ignore that."

"I can't give more than I have."

"But not less either."

"Was this that you wanted to tell me?" Mrs. Liebreich got up.

"There is still something else." Mrs. Pein hesitated. How could she break this shell? Did she dare too much? Maybe now I will lose everything. Then she said, "About the other house that belongs to this property. It's empty. I was told once it was reserved for guests. It could be renovated and perhaps converted into small apartments. One bedroom, two bedrooms, so everybody could have their own little home with bath and small kitchen. And then there could be a big concert hall as well."

"Ms Pein, don't forget, these are old people."

"People like you and I," Mrs. Pein said quietly.

Mrs. Liebreich bit her lips. Her eyes grew to a small slit. "Listen, I have already enough problems, more than I can handle, why should I create even more? It would be best if everything stays as it is. The old people got used to it, it worked so far, why should we change it? I don't see any necessity."

"It could be that the guests got used to it, but I got the impression, they have resigned to it. They don't have the strength to fight any more."

"I wish - -" Mrs. Liebreich did not finish the sentence.

"You wish I would give up too? Is that what you wanted to say? I have to disappoint you in that. I agree that we have different views of things, but I have to tell you also that we are paying guests. Therefore I believe we have a certain right."

"Do you want to threaten me?"

"Not at all! I would like to make you our ally, Mrs. Liebreich, that's all."

Mrs. Liebreich sat down again and leaned back in the chair. Mrs. Pein continued, "I don't think of old people only, but also young families. You know, the old people need the young and the young need the old people. Old people are like salt in the soup. If there is too much salt, you can't eat it. If it's too little, it doesn't taste good either. Everything has to be well balanced."

"Mrs. Pein, you are a dreamer."

"What is life without a dream."

"The reality is different."

"Did you never think that even a dream can become reality?"

"I wish I had something of your optimism."

"This I wish too," Mrs. Pein said and sighed.

"You are pretty stubborn. Has nobody told you that?"

Mrs. Pein smiled, "Not that I can remember." Then she added in a low voice, "yes, my daughter once told me that."

"What would this look like according to your fantasy?"

"This big building in the back. I looked from the outside. I did not know that a meadow and even a forest belongs to it. I only saw the yard plastered with the garbage cans. But there is far more to it. You know, this could become a little paradise. A park."

Mrs. Liebreich thought a while, then she opened a drawer. "The former owner once had some plans. They still must be somewhere here. But this is totally unrealistic. Who should do all the work?"

She closed the drawer again.

"Yes, it's a lot of work. But I am thinking how it would be when everything is finished."

"It would cost a fortune."

"Maybe it costs less than you think. Maybe we could even involve the old people, then they would see it as their property. Kind of a condo, that after their death would go back to the house. This all has to be regulated through a lawyer. Then the old people would have something to live for. This would give their lives a new meaning. It's the absence of meaning that makes it so difficult. The feeling nobody needs them any more and life goes on without them. I talked to many of them, more than just once. They are experienced in many ways, but nobody wants them. They are discouraged."

"I can't load another burden on my shoulders. Enough is enough."

"I believe it. It's far too much for one person. The load has to be shared, and for the construction work somebody else has to take responsibility, somebody who is experienced."

"You are talking as if this is already a set thing, Mrs. Pein. Forget it. Everybody is only interested in his or her own advantage."

"Not everybody, Mrs. Liebreich."

"Listen, I am not a charity. This is a hard business. It has to do with numbers. That's all that counts."

"Perhaps that's the mistake, Mrs. Liebreich. If you would think less of profit and more how to make the life for these people more worth living, your life would get a new meaning as well."

"If I would think of profit, I would double the price. But I ask again, who should do the work? And you are talking about the park. A park needs a gardener, and a house a caretaker. And who should do the job? These old people would not be able to."

"I know a gardener and a caregiver."

"This house can't afford any of those."

"The one I am thinking of does not even want a salary. He would be satisfied if he could live here and eat."

"I have to think this over. But it seems there is no end, of talking with you. Yesterday it was the canary, today the added house and what will come next?"

"Tomorrow will take care of itself."

"I admit, it's not all stupid, what you say." Mrs. Liebreich got up, also Mrs. Pein rose. "The house does not fit into this modern times, that's true. But apart from that, the concert was great. What was her name?"

"Judith Rosenstock."

"Rosenstock? Rosenstock? But not the well known pianist? My dear, if I had known that! I had no idea that she lived in our house."

"For nearly a year, Mrs. Liebreich. That's it, people in this home don't feel taken seriously by you. Somehow they feel exploited, used."

"Mrs. Pein be careful in what you say."

That night Mrs Pein lay awake most of the time. The conversation lay heavily on her. Again and again she repeated all the sentences and was wondering how she could be so bold. "If only I had never stepped into this office. I should not have asked her. But on the other hand, this was the best opportunity." Never before had she seen this kind of humanness.

"I should have been more careful in what I said. The door was a tiny slit open and maybe I closed it again."

She tried to shake off the conversation, but she could not. "Did I say too much? Did I hurt her? But somebody had to tell her, what everybody else was thinking."

Miss Baumgarten

March had passed. Still five more weeks to go, and as often as she started to count the weeks she had to admit that there was a fear still lingering. In the beginning she counted the days, hoping they would fly faster, and now she counted and realized that not many days were left any more.

Miss Baumgarten lay in bed and stared at the ceiling. Mrs. Pein got the impression she wanted to say something and was afraid to do so. But to be honest, right now Mrs. Pein did not want another talk. She was tired.

"That's strange, don't you think so too?" Miss Baumgarten started.

"Strange? What do you mean?"

"Life. You are lucky. When your daughter returns you can leave. You don't have to stay like me. If I would have a home, I could tolerate everything much easier. But here - this is all I have."

"It always depends what we are doing with a certain situation."

"You told me that hundreds of times already, but how, if I dare to ask? A person is fixed to his skin, he can't get rid of it, even if he wants to. No-no, that's not easy."

"A person is more than his skin."

"I don't deny this." Miss Baumgarten set up. "Do you listen at all? Mrs. Pein, for me it's a question of life and death."

Mrs. Pein undressed herself and hung her clothes into the wardrobe.

"Do you listen?"

"I listen, but I don't want to talk right now. I'm tired."

"But you have to! It's important. I don't have much time left. Therefore it's important." Mrs. Pein disappeared behind the curtain. One could hear the water running.

"The concert tonight," Miss Baumgarten raised her voice to be heard, "I haven't cried for years, but this evening I did, I cried like a baby. I didn't even know that I had tears left in my storage, but they could fill a whole bucket. Suddenly I thought, life could be so nice. Don't say anything. I just did not know it. I always thought life is gruesome. Life is my enemy. And so I treated it, as an enemy. But perhaps that's wrong. And this I don't understand. I don't understand myself any more."

Mrs. Pein put on the long light blue night-gown and opened the curtain, sat down in bed, bent her knees and pulled the cover up to her chin. Then she said, "Ten and a half years ago the doctors gave me half a year to live. They did not give me more. Since then I have lived on borrowed life. More then ten years long. And every day is not only a miracle for me, but a gift. Gift is not even the right word. It is - how shall I say? - it's a borrowed gift."

"That's not right. Either it's a gift or it isn't. A loan you have to pay back. A gift you can keep," Miss Baumgarten said.

"Still it's a borrowed gift. It belongs to me, but since it is borrowed, I can't do with it what I want. There is an obligation. To be precise, I am obliged to the one who gave it to me. Obliged is not the right word either, no it's not a suitable word. But I don't know any better. Maybe indebted to the giver out of gratitude. Sometimes, when I wake up in the morning and the darkness weighs me down, I think of all that I have and start to give thanks, for all those little things, one by one; and there is so much we can be thankful for."

"So, you too are familiar with the dark side of life? I always thought it was only me."

Mrs. Pein laughed. "If you would know! How often such a cloud creeps over me, a dark blanket, then I can't see the blue sky anymore. But then I tell myself, that this is not MY life, that I got it as a loan to do something with it, something meaningful. Just to wait for each meal, that's not enough."

"I understand. I feel the same. How long have you known this feeling, I mean this sadness?"

"Since - actually since my childhood. The first time this feeling came over me was when they took my father. I stood there and couldn't do anything. I saw how they treated him and then they took him away. They killed him. It was like I was paralysed."

"You never told me that."

"I know. We all live together side by side without knowing each other. Perhaps it's fear It's not easy to be so close together and then to talk about yourself. I mean about those inner feelings."

"If only I could know how to handle my own body," Miss Baumgarten said.

"Soon we won't need those old rags any more. Then we will look down on them and shake our head, asking ourselves how we could hold on to this that desperately for so long. "Lord teach me that we have to die," I never forgot how my father read these words. I was a child, maybe five or so - and still I remember. He read from a big book that was on his desk. I never forgot these words. When you are a child, you don't think of dying. However, we lived with death day by day. We were acquainted with him. And he gave our lives meaning. On that night our village burned. I was running desperately through the street not knowing where to turn. I tried to find the rest of my family. I never found them."

Mrs. Pein fell silent. Miss Baumgarten was also quiet. Finally Miss Baumgarten said in a hoarse voice, "I did not know. You never told me."

"You are right, maybe sometimes it would be easier if we would know more about each other. Then we would understand. Or maybe not. Who knows? But - it was a nice evening. And I believe something will change in this house."

"What do you mean?"

"After the concert I talked to Mrs. Liebreich."

"Don't mention her name. She is an old crow and always will be!"

"And what if we don't know her? Maybe she too is nothing but a hurting child. A child that is longing to be comforted."

"Comforted - she? Look how she is treating us. And we shall comfort her? Sorry, but I have to laugh. She wants our money, that's it. She is not even interested in one of us. She does not care if we peg out or not."

"These are hard words, Miss Baumgarten."

"Am I not correct?"

"I believe, we don't know her. Do you know that she cried this evening?"

"This dragon - cried? I have to laugh. To picture her crying makes me laugh!"

"After the concert."

"She was at the concert? I did not see her."

"She was very impressed and suggested we repeat such event, even in a bigger hall."

"I can't believe it! I am old and still there is something new to learn. No, I can't believe it!" After a short pause she continued, "I don't even miss the TV, I only realized it yesterday that it is no longer here. I had to laugh. I thought, without this glitter box I could not live. But life is much nicer without it."

155

"I am glad to hear that. I believe, television robs more than it gives."

"You are very religious, aren't you?"

"What do you mean?"

"Do you really believe that there is somebody up there?"

"Not only up there, also down here and everywhere. Yes, this I believe."

"I thought so. But why doesn't he do anything about all the bad things that are going on down here?"

"I am not his counsellor. He made heaven and earth and the whole universe, how shall I understand what he is doing or not doing."

"Do you believe, he has created all that?"

"This has not just happened by chance. There is a designer, a higher wisdom than we can imagine."

"This would be a big comfort to think that somebody knows what he is doing."

"Yes," Mrs. Pein said.

"Sometimes I am scared. You too?"

"More than you think."

"Not only for the future, for myself. I look into the mirror and suddenly I don't know myself anymore. I have become a stranger."

Mrs. Pein listened.

"Do you know that too? Sometimes when I look in the mirror I think there is a strange face looking at me."

"Sure, I know. But this is not important what we are from the outside."

"How nice this sounds."

Mrs. Pein was not sure if this was sarcasm or not.

"But this is our business card. That's me," Miss Baumgarten continued. "This face that we are carrying with us, this face with all those deep lines and shades - that's us - and yet it's not. But we are fixed to this wrapper, we can't just put it aside to take something better. It's always there. It sticks to us, even though we are painting it and try hard to change it, operate on it. Sometimes I hate this face. Then I want to run away. But it comes along, wherever I go. Yes, I want to run away, not to face myself anymore. I am afraid of myself.

I think, others are better, they have accomplished something - I can't show anything special. Then I tell myself, "you are a nothing, a nobody. An old woman that is worth nothing. Hardly anybody will follow your casket. There is nothing that could be said about you at the funeral. It could well remain un-lived. There is no difference, if I was there or not." No, don't say anything, I know that's true. You don't need to comfort me. Lets go to sleep, at least then I can forget."

Mrs. Pein could not sleep. This all was too much for her. First the conversation with Mrs. Liebreich, then with Miss Baumgarten, and she was just longing to be quiet. Her thought were with Britta and she was surprised that she did not miss her daughter.

She must have just fallen asleep, when a loud scream woke her up. Her heart pounded, as if it was about to burst. Her trembling finger fumbled for the light switch. With wide-open eyes she looked around. Where am I? Then she looked at Miss Baumgarten. She threw the bedcover back and tapped to the opposite bed. For a moment she waited at the foot end.

"Miss Baumgarten? Wake up!" She shook the bedcover. "You are dreaming!"

Miss Baumgarten groaned.

"It's all right," Mrs. Pein said, as if calming down herself. How familiar this was to her! How often she dreamed the same dream again and again. Wet from sweating she woke up each time. How could it be?" she asked herself.

Miss Baumgarten sat up and pulled at her night gown. "Do you have bad dreams too from time to time?"

"Yes."

"There I am that old already and still am persecuted by the shadows of the past. This I don't understand. Then I am afraid to go to sleep again. Do you know that too?"

Mrs. Pein nodded. "Life taught me a lot, and now I think, we have to have the courage to be nothing but a tiny seed, that is being put into the earth."

"You mean to die?"

"To bring fruit, yes. And this fruit is not for ourselves, it's nourishment for others. And in that we find at last our fulfilment."

"Miss Baumgarten was still sitting on the bed frame and looked down, then she said, "I did not tell you what happened in the hospital. In the bed beside me. We talked with each other. I asked something and she did not answer. And when I looked closer, I knew that she was gone. Like that. She was there and yet she was not there. She just left. Like that. Gone. Over. Like a soap-bubble. Nobody realized it. How could that be? I was wondering. The next morning I was scheduled for the operation. I thought, what will happen if I have to meet the Master. I was thinking what you told me, and I remembered one sentence, I am not sure, if you still remember or not. You read what Jesus once said to somebody, do you remember? "Who believes in me will live even though he dies." This sentence came to my mind suddenly. I thought I am getting insane. I am not religious as you know. But that night I took the New Testament out from the drawer of the night table and read, under the bedclothes with my flashlight, so nobody could see. I thought, if this would be true, then I would not need to be afraid of dying. Then death is nothing more than a threshold into a new life, a life without any shadow. But I am not sure. There are two worlds fighting each other, and I am not sure with which one I should befriend myself. Or are they not two? Is there only one? Oh, I guess, I get crazy. But I think, if I would have known that before, things would have been different."

Mrs. Pein waited to see if Miss Baumgarten would continue. Her glance fell on the low night table. There she saw the book *Stories and even more stories*. Mrs. Pein took it and turned over the leaves.

"Do you know the stories of the wild geese?"

"I read it once, maybe you could read it again, I really liked it. Could you?"

Mrs. Pein sat down on the bed and read:

The migration of the geese

Once there lived an old man at the edge of a pasture who could understand the language of the animals. His little hut was exactly where a small vaulted bridge went across a brook. And in front of the hut was a bench, marked by the weather. On this bench the old man was sitting watching the wild geese, strutting over the meadow looking for food. Every evening he was sitting there on the weather-beaten bench at the edge of the big meadow talking to the animals, and the animals talking to him, until the day when they moved on. He waited year after year for their return. And when they gathered to prepare for their long journey, he knew they would come back. Then he followed them with his eyes, listening to their wailing cries and was tormented by an indescribable sadness. And yet he could not even tell why this sadness came over him. Was it because they went away, those, who became his friends? Or was it because he could not follow them and he did not even know where they were driven to go. Did they not have everything they needed? What else could he have given them? Then he comforted himself with the idea that they will come back next spring.

But one day they did not come back. The old man waited and waited. And one evening he thought as if he had seen in the far distance one of the wild geese. He uttered his familiar cry, and indeed the bird answered and came closer. But he was on his own.

"Where are your companions?" the old man asked.

"They stayed."

"Why did they not come along," he wanted to know.

"You know, old man, as long as we live we are driven by a hidden longing, as if deep within us would be left a vague idea of a distant light. But so far we have not found this light, as much as we looked for it. And yet it once lived in us and now it drives us from place to place. A bright light that stayed in our memory, a light that filled everything. So we flew towards the light, year after year, always hoping to find it again. But we never found what still lived in us. Until now.

When we left this place we found the One who created us. After that we did not want to come back. Then we all knew that it was He whom we were searching for all those years, it was He after whom we were longing without knowing. When we saw Him, we did not want to leave. Only I came back to look if one of us is still here. But they all followed us. Finally we found peace. Finally we are at home.

Mrs. Pein put the book back and shut off the light. The first glimmer of grey waited behind the curtain. A bird tried timidly his first song.

"O Lord who has created Heaven and earth, enlighten this world," she prayed silently.

The next morning she wanted to get up but a heavy weariness forced her to lay down. Her head was hammering. Was she sick? She looked at the bed beside her. It was empty. She pulled the bed sheet above her ears. Sometimes she wished to shed off this life like an old sick skin.

Suddenly she remembered something that she had read somewhere, "Even if the outer man falls apart, the inner one is renewed day by day." Was it not the great apostle who said that? Then there was hope after all. She thought about the conversation from last night. What was the secret?

When the spirit of God, who raised Jesus from the dead lives within us - - from where did these words come? Did he live in her? To let go of herself. To surrender to the One who is bigger. There was still so much to learn. Would she ever arrive that she could say, now I arrived? No, she always would remain a learner. As long as she was on her way. And that was good also. She would never hold something in her hands saying, that's what I've accomplished. She was depending on mercy. She was like a child, that was peeking through the keyhole on Christmas eve and could only guess a tiny bit about the beauty that lay behind that door. What would it be when the door opened?

"Mrs. Pein", she heard the voice of Miss Baumgarten beside her bed, "are you sick?"

Mrs. Pein tried to sit up. "I'm all right, this will pass."

"I brought breakfast for you." Miss Baumgarten put the tray on the night table. "I talked a lot last night, sorry. But thanks anyway, it helped. If only you won't leave. I don't know what I would do without you. Are you sure that your daughter is coming on the sixth?"

Mrs. Pein nodded.

"That's in a couple of days already..."

Farewell from the old people's home

It was May 5th. In the yard beams and boards were piled up, spring flowers stretched their delicate stalks enfolding their beauty. Heavy equipment had been brought in. Men in their helmets were running back and forth. One could hear hammering, sawing and drilling. The old people watched fascinated the progress of the construction. And in the evening when the workers had left, the old people secretly sneaked onto the building site, to see the progress. *Keep out, trespassing strictly forbidden.* But they did not pay any attention to the big signs everywhere. The big bright staircase was covered with cardboard so not to cause any damage. One could even see some of the apartments with large windows and a bathroom and even a small kitchen. And in the first floor there were the guest rooms, but they were not ready yet. Ladders, pots of paint and all kind of utensils were standing around. The best thing however was the big hall with high windows which would catch the sun. Soon this would become their new home. They could hardly wait. They even would be allowed to bring their own furniture, and those who did not have any could get some from the house. The wing to the left was for young families. "Life has to be experienced," Mrs. Liebreich had said. But of course, there were certain regulations that should be followed - like hours of rest - to make the togetherness possible.

Jan helped Mrs. Pein to cross a bridge of boards. "This will be my apartment," he said proudly and encouraged Mrs. Pein to come closer. From the window she could see a large meadow, framed by high trees. The sinking sun laid a golden vale over the cherry trees, decorating them with diamonds. She could see the first signs of new life everywhere. Soon also other trees who had slept their long sleep would be awake, enfolding their beauty, like a bride's veil.

"Over there could be our vegetable garden," she heard Jan's voice, "then we will have fresh vegetables every day. Do you know, what is still missing?" he asked and continued, "a little store, like our village store. I was wondering, if Miss Graser would be willing to open such a store here as she did in our village? Old people always need something to give as a present, maybe to their grandchildren, little things, and things they would need for every day living. Then they would not need to go far."

Mrs Pein did not say anything. She was very quiet. Tomorrow her daughter would come to bring her home. Tomorrow of all days. Just now when everything has started to change.

"In a couple of weeks every thing will be ready, one of the workers told me. I have already packed my things. I don't have much. And I will also have my own workroom, the heat is already in. We have to prepare this year again for the Gingerbread House. I never thought that we would sell that much! My brother said, nobody sold as much as we did."

This night Mrs. Pein could not sleep. Miss Baumgarten had to go again to the hospital for an examination and was supposed to be back around noon. Mrs. Pein was on her own. She slipped on her dark housecoat, the buttons at the top were left open, so the light blue night-gown could shine through. Her throat showed deep lines, Her eyes red from crying. The thin white hair was hanging unkempt to the shoulders. Her hands trembled. Why on earth was she going to give up all that? She tried to remember how it was in the village where she lived before. Many of those who she once knew where no longer there. She would be very lonely, the more since even Jan would not be there any more.

Britta would be at work the whole day. The village store is no longer there. And Helena would not come to feed the ducks. "What is left there for me?"

She stared at the door. The dried wreath was still hanging at the door. A draught played with the red ribbon.

Here always was somebody to whom I could talk. "What am I going to do in the village?" she started to talk to herself and finished packing the last things into her suitcase and looked once more into the storage room. There all the boxes were tidily packed. Jan had helped her, just like before. Somebody will come to get them later on. Now she took her blue-white striped dress out of the wardrobe and put it on. She brushed her hair. Finally she took her coat and the big dark straw hat and looked at the watch. She did not want Britta to wait. She should be here any moment.

"Hansi!" she said, "I nearly forgot you!"

She put the suitcase in front of the door and went to the lounge to get the birdcage. "My little friend, now we are going back again, where we came from." At first she wanted to say, we are going back home - but somehow it was not her home any more. "You felt quite at home here, haven't you? With your beautiful singing you spread so much joy. You never sang that much as in the last couple of days. As often as Mrs. Rosenstock played the piano, you accompanied her with your singing. You were a nice team!"

She took the cage. The little bird fluttered anxiously up and down.

"Don't be afraid, I am with you. The two of us will stick together, won't we?"

When she arrived at the entrance hall, nearly all the house guests were gathered. Bewildered she looked around. Was something going on that she did not know about? Then she saw Britta. Her daughter came running and embraced her. The cage swayed back and forth and the bird fluttered desperately.

"Be careful, look at the bird!" she warned her daughter.

"Is that how you are greeting me?" her daughter asked partly annoyed, partly jokingly. "I thought you could not wait to see me." Then she looked at all the stern faces. "What happened?" she asked in a muffled tone.

"Nothing."

"Because you are leaving?"

"I am not sure."

At that moment Helena came with her teddy clutched in her arms.

"Aunt Pein are you coming back soon?"

Britta took the bird cage. "I'll take this to the car in the meantime. Where is your suitcase?"

"In front of my door."

Britta went to the car to put the cage in safely, then came back, sprang up the stairs, for it took too long to wait for the elevator.

"Are you coming back soon?" Helena asked again, tears in her eyes.

Mrs. Pein wiped her eyes, while her right hand stroked the curly hair of her little friend.

"This all became part of me," she said in a low voice. "Here we cried and laughed together. It is strange how people can grow together. Everything was cold and grey, but now it's warm and familiar."

"Much has changed, Mrs. Pein," Mrs. Liebreich said.

"Yes, much has changed. But I think not only from the outside, also within something has changed," Mr. Guttman said. Mrs. Rosenstock smiled and pressed his hand.

The elevator opened. Britta stepped out, in her hand the black suitcase. This time she had used the elevator.

"Are you coming, mother?"

Mrs. Pein hesitated. She saw Jan. He was standing aside, pressing his cap. "And soon the baby would be born and I am not here," Mrs. Pein thought. "And what about Helena?"

"We will miss you," Mrs. Liebreich said.

"I probably will miss you more than you miss me."

"This house has changed."

"You know, there are problems we can't solve. Problems that are stay with us through all our life like a chain that is fixed to us. But sometimes there are problems, they just fall off like a ripe fruit from the tree. And I believe this all was such a ripe fruit, that fell into our hands. I didn't do anything. I was afraid. Yes, I was afraid. In the beginning I often thought of running away. Then I told myself, Pein one does not run away before trying everything.

But I was not alone. There was especially Jan. This all would not have happened if it wouldn't have been through him. He was the one who stood at my side to encourage me, and I knew I could rely on him."

Jan was still standing in the dark corner, the squeezed cap in his hands. His eyes were shining. He wiped them secretly with a clean handkerchief, then again he pressed his old cap and took out the dents and pressed it again. This cap was a part of him.

"And Toni our cook. Since Toni took charge of the kitchen, the large sign is gone: *Keep out.* Instead there is now a sign at the door with a large heart and there you can read *Let yourself be surprised.* And then Sister Hanna. It was not always easy for her. But her laughter often gave us new courage."

She looked from one to the next. "Helena - what a pleasure it was to have her around, how much joy did she bring to this place!"

Outside a car was honking. It was Herbert.

"Mother, I just can't understand," Britta said growing more and more impatiently.

"Britta, please wait, just a bit longer so I can say good-bye."

"You don't want to come?"

Miss Baumgarten came with two men from the ambulance and was startled.

"You are leaving? Mrs. Liebreich can't you tell her to stay? What should become of us?" She started to cry.

"Are you coming or not?" Britta asked.

Mrs. Pein shook slowly her head. "You know, I got so used to everything here. And here there is always somebody I can talk with. You are away the whole day. If I think it over, it would be best to stay."

"Mother, I really don't understand. I came here for your sake. I often felt guilty leaving you alone, even though they offered me a job for another year or even longer."

"And? Did you accept?"

"Not yet. I did not dare."

"Would you have liked to do so?"

"Oh mother, something like that had always been my dream. One year in America, do you know what that means for me?"

"Why then didn't you accept?"

"Mother, what on earth happened with you?"

"I don't know myself, Britta. No, I can't understand myself. Maybe I would like to do both, to be with you and to stay. For one year, you said?"

"From next month."

"Why don't you call and tell them that you are coming?" I could then rent a small apartment here with my own furniture, then we both would be happy. What do you think?"

Britta embraced her mother with force. Mrs. Pein saw tears in the eyes of her daughter.

"Is it that bad?" she asked jokingly.

"Mother, I can't tell you how happy I am."

"And if I am happy, you don't care?"

"Are you?"

Mrs. Pein nodded. "I would never have thought so."

Jan came closer. He had heard everything. Now he beamed with joy.

"You are staying?"

Mrs. Pein smiled sheepishly.

"Then let's start," he said.

"Yes, let's start," Mrs. Pein answered.